UNDER THE
MAGPIE'S WINGS

UNDER THE MAGPIE'S WINGS

JANA MEADOR

Copyright © 2015 Jana Meador
All rights reserved.

ISBN-10: 0988904497
ISBN-13: 9780988904491

ISBN 978-0-9889044-6-0
ISBN 978-0-9889044-7-7

Printed in the United States of America.

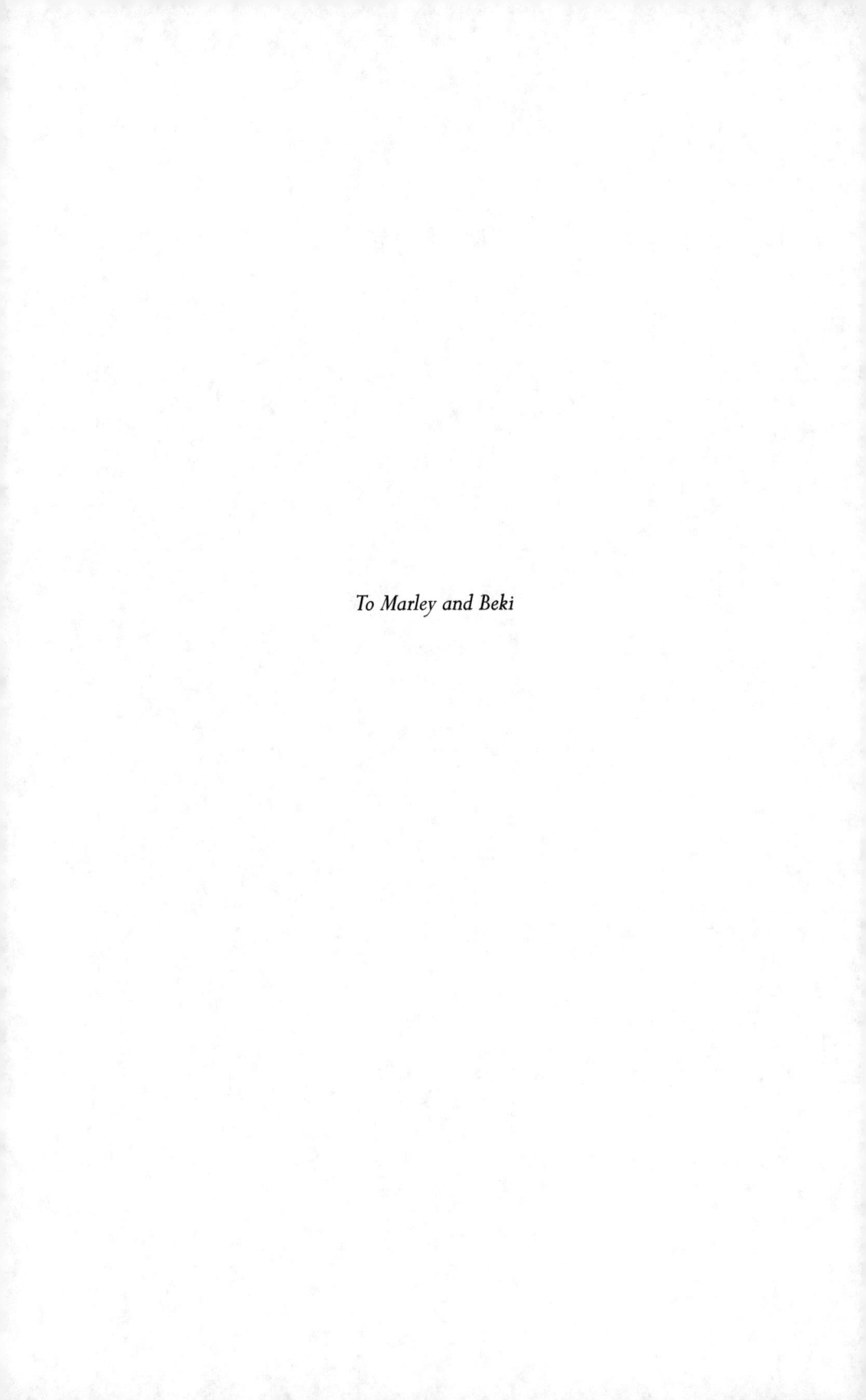

To Marley and Beki

Chapter 1

MONTANA, 1915

J ust at the end of the road where it forks lay the small, but not forgotten town Wiley. Surrounded by tall Rocky Mountains on one side and the wide, cold waters of the Agate River on the other, the valley spread out for miles and flourished with vast fields and meadows filled with bright colorful flowers. Butterflies flew over the plains and bumblebees buzzed in the air while some nested in the blooms of the wild plants. The mountain hare hopped over the grass and carelessly nibbled on the patch of forest strawberries. The sun beams shined through the tall spruce and pine branches, and the birds worked tirelessly on their eyries, soon to welcome their young ones. The warm breeze moved through the pastures and lifted up high, leaving several rings behind on the surface of Hidden Lake in the mountain saddle.

Marco enjoyed hard work on the fields. No matter the weather outside, the animals needed to be fed, cleaned and taken care of. The pregnant cow had been in labor for about three hours. Vin Savelli knew he has to step in to help the cow deliver her calf. This time, he called his grandson for help. Marco was ten years old, and Vin suggested it was the right time to introduce him to this kind of job. He knew Marco has developed a deep sense of love for farm animals, just like him, when he was at his age, and his father taught him the peeves and perks of the farm life. But for most, Vin absolutely loved and adored his only grandson.

Marco inherited his Italian genes; he had a perfect olive complexion, and was slim and tall, much taller than other ten year olds. He had dark brown eyes and curly, raven-colored hair. When they got to the barn, the cow was laying down, surrounded by straw. She was breathing heavily, with her stomach bloated.

"Magpie, go get the cow's tail and hold it straight up. Hurry," Vin ordered as he himself knelt down behind the cow. He slid his hand right inside and checked the unborn calf. "Still breathing, but we have to get it out quick. Time is running out for the little one. Hand me the chains." Vin said loudly.

Marco, still holding the cow's tail, reached for the chains.

"Thanks Magpie, now, get out of my way!" Vin ordered sharply.

Marco got up and took a few steps back. His eyes had never left the pregnant cow. He continued watching his grandfather as Vin's arm reached inside the cow again, and pulled out the calf's two legs. Then he took the chain and made two loops around the hooves.

"Now, come on up here, and help me pull the little one out!"

Marco's feet took slow steps forward as he joined Vin and grabbed the cold chain. They pulled hard and then pulled again. The cow started pushing as they were pulling. Vin felt the sweat breaking on his forehead.

"Come on!" he yelled and then the little black and white miracle came out, but it wasn't breathing. Marco watched as his grandfather opened the newborn calf's mouth and tried to get the membrane out, then he pulled on her tongue to the point it hanged out of its mouth.

"Where's the bucket?" he asked and quickly looked around.

Marco rushed to the bucket that was filled with ice cold water. He lifted it, but it was too heavy for him to carry it to his grandfather. Vin got up and helped him with it.

"Pour the water over the calf's head. Like this, see?!" Vin turned the bucket upside down and all the water splashed over the calf's head and face. The baby calf started breathing immediately.

"Grandpa, look!" Marco cheerfully pointed his finger toward the baby calf.

"It shocks them; the cold water shocks them, and it always works!" Vin looked at the newborn calf. "Good job, Magpie. I am very proud of you. You delivered your first cow today!" He wrapped his arms around Marco shoulders.

"See, that's a good sign. She accepted her calf. Come on, let's leave them alone now." The old Italian placed his other arm around his young grandson's shoulder as they headed out of the barn into the midday sun. "You gotta give her a name…"

With a proud smile on his face, Marco replied, "Milly." He felt all grown up, and it brought him a step closer to become a farmer just like his grandfather. That's all the ten year old ever wanted.

"Are you hungry now?"

"I'm starved." They exited the barn and walked across the yard toward the house. Isabel greeted her son with a kiss on his cheek. She served them breakfast and listened to her father as he talked in excitement about the adventure they endured earlier in the morning.

"I'm very proud of your boy; he delivered his first calf today," Vin said as he took a bite out of a piece of bread.

"I only helped *you*, grandpa."

"No, you did a whole lot more than just help. Without the bucket of ice cold water there would be no calf today."

His grandfather started calling him *Magpie* the day he was born. Vin told him a story, that on that very same day, when he arrived, there was a magpie sitting on a branch outside of the window. The magpie did not move all day and night. It just sat there and watched baby Marco in his crib. At first, Marco's mom, Vin's daughter, worried about her baby. After all, magpies are known for stealing things. True, the things magpies like to take are usually shiny and glittery, but to her, her newborn baby was just like that. A little golden nugget, the most precious gem, wrapped in a white blanket. When Vin came to see his newborn grandson, she told him about the bird outside of the window. Vin laughed it off, but then even he was curious about the magpie. They tried to scare it off, but the bird would always return and sit on the same exact pine branch. While they gave up chasing it away after a while, the bird did never give up. Vin assumed it must be a sign. And from that day forward, he started calling his little grandson Magpie. Over the years, the bird on the branch would eventually return, and they all could see him here and there. As Marco grew older, Vin became the only person, who still persistently called him by his nickname. This made Marco feel special. He knew he felt a lot closer to his grandfather than to his own father. While his grandpa was a tall, strong man of his word, his father was a total opposite. Vin often called him *a loser*. "There is only one word that defines you! But there is never too late to change that, remember that!"

"You've got a great son, Isabel. He's got our genes. The only genes that are worth anything..."

"Dad! Shh, please don't...." Isabel shook her head. She knew where the conversation would go. She stopped it right in time.

"You are a great cook, Isabel. You took after your mother. She was a great cook. I miss her a lot."

"I miss her too, Dad." Isabel reached with her hand over the table and pressed his hand. She felt his rough skin in her palm. She gently kneaded his thick, knuckled fingers. Vin had been a farmer since he was child. She wasn't sure if she wanted her only son Marco to follow the same path. Farm work meant hard labor. She pictured her son to go to school, to have an education, perhaps become a doctor or a lawyer. But this was very distant to Isabel, who spent her entire life on the farm, on the outskirts of small, Montana town called Wiley.

"Where's your husband, Isabel?" Vin's deep voice echoed through the kitchen.

"Dad, not in front of Marco..." She tilted her head toward her son at the table.

"Does he even realize how much he has been missing by not being here? I mean, look at Magpie. Look at him, what a great, young man he's become! While his father is getting drunk every day God knows where!"

"Grandpa, it's okay," said Marco.

"No, it's not okay. But you are too little to understand it." Vin put the last spoonful of soup in his mouth. He wiped the corners of his lips with his shirt. He tapped his grandson's shoulder, got up and kissed his daughter's cheek. Without saying another word, Vin exited the house.

"Does dad likes us?" Marco asked timidly.

Isabel saw the sadness in her son's eyes. "Yes, I think he likes us." The sound of her voice betrayed her. She wasn't a good liar. "Go play now." She kissed his raven hair and removed the empty plates from the table.

✦

His curiosity got the most out of him. He had to go back to the barn to check on Milly. Now, the calf was several hours old. She stood next to her mother, feeding on milk. Marco watched behind a wooden fence. He dared to move, to make a noise. Milly thrived, getting stronger by the hour. He thanked his grandfather; if not for him, the calf wouldn't be alive. Sometimes he wished the day had more hours, because he had so much to learn. The little boy admired the wisdom his grandfather had. Everything he knew, he had learned himself through his stubborn persistence and willingness. Vin had only basic education; he could read and write, but it didn't stop him to further gain the wisdom through life lessons. Marco knew his mother's wish would be to stay in school as long as possible. She had always told him that the more education you have the easier life you can make for yourself. People will pay you more respect. But Marco was still a 10-year-old child. He didn't understand all the adult talk. Since his father hadn't been present much, it was his grandfather who filled in the spot and became his mentor and best friend. He didn't mind the physical work, what else was there to do? When school was over for the day, he would come home, eat something little and then start helping on the farm. Whether it was on the field, or around the animals, the manual work just made him happy. Vin could see the joy in Marco's eyes.

Now, the baby cow got tired and laid down, curling next to her mama. Marco threw some grain to the chickens and their three-colored rooster. The bird was rather old and small but very vocal, which gained him respect among his hens. It was the leader of the pack, quite intelligent, and the rooster restlessly watched over his queens. So, the Savelli decided to let the rooster live for as long as it would last. Now, at his old age, there wasn't much beauty left on him. He had a limp and his voice got somewhat squeaky. Two days ago, Vin came by to cut the rooster's claws. They were getting too long and were growing into back of his legs. While Marco held him, Vin took the sheep's scissors to cut the thick, hard nails.

"You cut too much, and he will start bleeding; you cut too little, and it won't be enough to do the job." Vin said, holding the big loops of sheep scissors in his hand.

"How do you know where to cut, Grandpa?"

"You don't. You cut and you see what happens. If it starts bleeding, we have to wrap it up, so the rooster doesn't get infection in his leg."

"I can't hold him much longer, grandpa, look; he is all twitching and turning in my lap..."

"Flip him on his back. When the bird is on his back, he'll stop moving." Vin set the large scissors on the ground. He got up and flipped the bird in Marco's lap. "Like this. See, now he is calm. I don't know what it is about the birds, but as soon as they are on their back, they become *relaxed*."

"Wow, it really works," Marco said cheerfully.

Vin cut the rooster's claws, and they didn't bleed a bit.

"See, walking don't hurt him no more!" Vin laughed.

The bird rushed to join his hens, who welcomed their one and only king.

"Next time you can do it all by yourself, Magpie!" he added quickly.

Vin lived nearby his daughter's house on the same farm land. When his daughter married, he gave her a half of the land and the main house. Then he moved into a smaller place that he had built by himself. The two houses were divided by a pond that held several types of small fish. Marco would catch the fish for fun and then release it back to the pond. He let the wild birds feed on it. When he got older and realized that the pond froze over the winter, the boy worried the fish would die. This took some explaining and persuading to make him believe the fish would be just fine and when the spring comes, it will be swimming from one end of the pond to the other. Marco liked the spring time. He enjoyed watching the transition the nature made from cold, snowy and somewhat quiet winter into the warm and colorful picture around him. The birds would slowly return and fill the air with their songs, while tirelessly building their nests for their future newborns. The life became richer and gained new purpose. The animal instinct kicked in. The farmer's boy lay in the grass. He crossed his arms behind his head and stared at the blue sky.

Chapter 2

MONTANA, 1925

Marco often sat in the grass by the pond. He looked up at the sky where several white scattered clouds floated and their reflection showed in warm water in front of him. The green grass moved in the breeze and the branches of an old apple tree arched over the surface of the nearby barn. He spent hours watching the birds, listening to their lovely songs when they finally arrived to their summer destination. He looked forward to this season as much as he was just a 10-year-old boy, just like now, a decade later, a young, 20-year-old grandson of an Italian immigrant, still fascinated by the undeniable beauty Montana had to offer. Soon after a pack of mallard ducks flew overhead, he looked up against the sky, his right hand shielding his forehead from the midday sun. The ducks made a loop in the air and flew back, landing on the pond in front of him. One duck after another spread their wings, and with their bright orange feet they hit water, and broke on the surface until they stopped, folding their wings and shaking their feathered tails. Marco wondered where they came from. The ducks never stayed over the winter. They couldn't, because they would freeze to death and there just wasn't' enough to eat for them. The Rocky Mountain Montana winters always brought a lot of snow, with wind and blizzards. These ducks needed an open water to live. Ever since he was a little boy, every fall, he would come up waiting for the ducks and geese to appear to say goodbye to them. He would repeat this until one day, the ducks would not come. The mallards and Canadians were finally on their way to their winter habitat.

"They flew south," Vin said softly. "They ain't gonna be back any time soon."

When Marco was a teenager he wished they would take him with them. Some place into the unknown, some place south. But that was then. Seemed like a long time ago. And now, Marco watched as the ducks started feeding on the underwater plants. They flew thousands of miles and were exhausted. The water and the bottom of the pond offered exactly, what the birds needed. He remembered what his grandpa told him. The plants underwater were covered in allergens-rich nutrients. Amongst others, it also provided them with sodium, which Vin explained was basically salt for all the birds. Marco reached for a stable of tall grass, ripped it off the ground and placed it in his mouth. He started chewing on it. When he was younger he did this to imitate Vin's pipe.

"Don't get into this habit, Magpie," Vin said firmly.

"But I want to be just like you, grandpa," the little boy replied.

Marco's lips curled into a smile, uncovering a white row of teeth. Where did all that time go? One of the male ducks swam directly to feet. Carefully watching the only human, that made the ducks a company, by the round pond, and under the large cottonwood tree. Suddenly, Marco got up and rolled up his pants, taking off his shoes and with his bare feet he stepped into the water. The mallard duck blissfully ignored him. He extended his arm toward the duck's beak. The duck's neck did the same, became longer and curious with his human companion. The wild bird started nibbling on Marco's fingers, making him laugh. The tingling sensation went through his entire body. He heard other birds singing in the background as if they were a part of this connection. The serene atmosphere didn't last long. The drunken, violent voice came from behind and stormed up like an unchained hurricane.

"What do you think you are doing, son? Huh? What is this?" Walter Wagner threw his arms in the air and shrugged his narrow shoulders. He was drunk. Marco felt his heartbeat go up. The scared male mallard duck quickly followed the rest of the group. The birds pushed themselves from the water and into the air and flew away. "I said what are you doing here?"

Walter Wagner's face grew sweaty and red. The unleashed evil alcohol had already consumed his entire soul.

"I'm just hanging out....Not doing anything, really..."

"Hanging out....with the bunch of ducks! My son is HANGING OUT with bunch of ungrateful ducks!" He extended his arm toward Marco, and then he raised his hand into the air. He aimed an invisible gun at the bird in the sky, as his imagination pushed the trigger.

"Pow! That's what you should be doing with these ducks...!" Wagner yelled disgustedly. Before he could continue his right foot got hitched over his left ankle. The drunk fell onto the ground.

"Shit! Help me up!" yelled Wagner. "What are you waiting for, I said help me up!"

Marco's instinct kicked in. He turned around and started running. He ran across the grass, around the pond and didn't stop until he made sure his evil father wasn't anywhere near his back.

❖

"Oh my God, he is beautiful!" Annie stroked the horse's nose.

"I am glad you like him. Happy birthday, my princess!" Charles Newman hugged his only daughter. The mare was brown and white, and cowboys called it *the paint horse*. Its saddle was white on the top of her back. "Her name is Digby." Charles placed the horses' rains into Annie's soft hands. Digby waggled its ears and the annoying flies flew above the horse's head.

"Digby," Annie whispered kissing the mare's nose. She had been riding horses ever since she was five years old.

"I thought you might want a new friend since you are now eighteen and won't need us anymore."

"Oh, father, she is gorgeous! Wish, mother could come and see Digby herself." Annie hugged her father again. She wrapped her arms around his neck so tight, that he almost couldn't breathe. "All right, all right, Annie." He laughed happily. The Newmans arrived in Wiley a week ago. Still too early to tell, but Annie found herself liking the small, somewhat lost town in the Rocky

Mountains. It was he mother, she worried about. Despite Elizabeth's beautiful spirit, the woman carried a terrible scar with her. Annie grew very protective of her mother and hoped she can adjust to the new environment quickly. The town was settled in the valley, and surrounded by mountain peaks on each side. The warm breeze brushed over Elizabeth's cheeks as she sat in a lawn chair on her new patio. The sun was about to go down, to hide behind the tall peaks. The sky lit with a various colors of red, orange and yellow. Perhaps it wept bloody tears, for Elizabeth, who watched the sunset through her blind eyes. She closed her eyelids and pointed her head toward the red sky.

"The sun's going down now; it'll be just a moment., " Charles stood behind Elizabeth's chair. He wrapped his arms around her slim shoulders. She brought his palms into hers and gently kissed his right hand.

"Is Annie back yet?" she asked.

"She took the horse for a ride." Charles kissed the top of his wife's head.

"The sun went down for the day," said Elizabeth and Charles looked up at the sky and replied, "It's time to go inside."

Early in the morning, when the grass was covered with dew, and there were no mountain hares to chase each other in the tall, brushy stables of the endless Montana meadows, Annie opened her eyes, and stretched her arms behind her head. She stood up taking several steps toward the window, moving the curtains to the sides and letting the fresh air in as she looked at the slow rising sun on the sky. She dressed in pants and a linen shirt and headed to the barn. The girl learned at her young age, what it took to own and keep such large animal. Her little hand would often hold a brush, her feet climbed on a wooden bench to reach on the top of the horse's back, waiting and excepting to be brushed. The stable's employees needed to keep an eye on her, even though she didn't want anyone to help her. A little girl's stubborn mind always won.

"Horses can kick," an employee said cautiously. "Never stand behind one, unless the horse is familiar with you and you feel comfortable with him."

Annie's long, braided blonde hair was tied in the back of her head into a ponytail, leaving just few loose strands around her forehead.

"You are up early," her father greeted her, as she walked out of the stable with her horse.

"I couldn't sleep."

"Did you worry about Digby?"

"No. Just wanted to make the best out of this day and start it early, I guess. Is mother still asleep?"

"Yes, Annie, she is. She is very happy you like Digby so much. It was the horse she picked for you." Charles Newman watched his daughter ride into the brand new dawn. Holding a mug of hot coffee, he took a sip and returned back to the house. His mind shifted to his wife of twenty years. Elizabeth Newman was a noble woman. Born in Louisiana, she was the only child of George and Mary Coleman. They owned a plantation where they grew cotton. They also had stables with horses, which Mrs. Mary Coleman rode for fun. Elizabeth soon discovered her own empathy and love for these four-legged beauties. When she met Charles, she knew this was a love at first sight! Elizabeth didn't care about the jewelry; she had a different wish for her future husband. She wanted to have her own stables. Charles, on the other hand, knew nothing about raising and owning horses. But he was willing to learn and educate himself, because the reward he gained was more than worth it to him. He married the love of his love and moved her into the Midwest, where he purchased a 500-acre estate. There was plenty of space for the new stables and enough horses to make his wife happy for a lifetime! Naturally, when Annie was born two years later, her mother brought her into the stables and told her, that even if the life throws stones at you, the horses will always be there for her. They will always accept her; no matter if she is happy or sad, and they will help her to overcome any burden life can bring. Later Elizabeth told that people may betray her but horses will never do such thing. From that day forward, Elizabeth and her little daughter shared mutual love for these noble animals. Life was great for them, until the time had come when Elizabeth felt ill with Scarlett fever. The prognosis wasn't good. When Charles heard the devastating news, he couldn't possibly bring himself to tell Annie that her mother had become blind. Annie was just seven years old. He remembered the day when Annie asked him to help walk her mom to the stables. Now, the picture was in his mind, as if it happened just yesterday. On that rainy day, the family was together in the living room. Annie got up and said she wanted to go to see the horses. Charles had told her that the weather outside was pretty bad and that she would be soaked by the time she got to the stables. She replied she didn't mind the rain and that she still wanted to take her mother to the stables. A calf was born earlier that day. Charles helped his wife together with Annie to the stables. There, at that time, seven-year-old Annie took her mother's hand and placed it onto the horse's nozzle.

"The horses will always be here for you, Mommie!" Annie said as she watched her blind mother's hand to go over the mare's face. The newborn calf stood just next to the big horse, watching the humans, and then moving under the mother's belly to get her milk.

The memory brought tears into Charles's eyes as it did a year ago when they all stood there in the barn on that rainy day. There was no cure for Scarlett fever and this was the bitter toll Elizabeth paid. Was Charles too selfish to wish to safe his wife, despite the fact she may never see again? When his wish came true, and Elizabeth survived the deadly fevers, Charles wanted to be the blind one. He retrieved to happier times, like when Elizabeth picked the new wallpaper for their dining room at the old house. The women passed the dining room. Elizabeth looked at the wallpaper that decorated the three walls. She picked a combination of light green and white colored stripes. There were various wild birds on painted branches. One could think, they competed who's got the best colored feathers, like the Western Meadowlark, a medium-sized bird, whose belly got brightest yellow feathers. The bird's head, a combination of black and white cropped colors made the Meadowlark look unique, so did the rest of the top of his feathers. There was a patch of pure black feathers in the middle of his chest, under his grey, sharp beak. A visible line on each side from the black patch, making it look as if the Western Meadowlark wore a black diamond necklace. They have seen it outside of their property; these birds thrived in the part of Montana where they lived. Although this bird eats mostly insect, they also could be seen picking up on berries and seeds. They nested in high grass and sometimes put their eggs in danger, when the time came to cut the grass. Elizabeth had a big heart for horses and birds. She spent hours educating herself, reading books and showing the colored pictures to her husband Charles, and later when their daughter was born, she would teach Annie everything she has learned about the wild birds in Montana. The next bird on the wallpaper was called Eastern Bluebird. As the name predicted, the small bird carried such a beautiful, rich blue color. Males had their tails, backs, wings, and heads colored blue like the sky on a bright, sunny day. Their bellies were a combination of chestnut and snowy white color with a black little feet and black, small, but very sharp beak. The females had similar colors but not that distinct. The Bluebird liked to feast on various kinds of food it could find in low vegetation, grass and meadows. They enjoyed eating grasshoppers, moths, caterpillars and also spiders. The bird was incredibly fast, pretty blue predator. The next bird on the wallpaper was an Eastern Kingbird. The grey-black bird with white underpants, long tails, and pointed wings always flew in flocks. Their Latin name was *Tyrranus Tyrranus* for a reason. Although the bird averaged in around 7 to 9 inches longs, there was nothing that would scare him off easily. Tyrranus would viscously defend its nest up, usually built up high on poles, or branches of the shrubs and trees. This bird would go without a fear against much larger birds in order to defend its eggs and its own territory. But there was one more bird the Newman's shared their dining room with. That bird was Ash-Throated Flycatcher. Elizabeth thought the bird's same was so ironic. He belonged to the Tyrant family, just like the Bluebird. The Flycatcher rarely caught its prey while in the air. These birds were ground hunters. They would quickly snatch the insects from the foliage or underground. Sometimes they would catch small mice and snakes. When that happened, the bird would beat the prey on the ground until dead. That's why the Flycatcher belonged to the Tyrant family. The colors on the bird weren't as pretty as the Bluebird's or the Western Meadowlark's. There wasn't even a significant color difference between the sexes. The males and the females both had short and bushy crest, pale yellow bellies, their backs were various shades of brown and their chest and throat had light gray color. There was a reason this bird wasn't bright yellow, blue or red. With the shades of brown and gray and pale yellow, the Flycatcher blended on the ground, thus the prey catching was easier for this type of wild bird. The wallpaper had many other and a lot bigger bird species, such as Red-tailed Hawk, an Eagle, and also a Canadian goose or a prairie falcon.

Charles once joked that they are the only house inviting all sorts of birds to watch them dine in the whole Montana state.

"What happened to pots, and pans, and silverware? Wouldn't you rather have apples and cherries on the wall here?"

"No, I would not, Charles. I'd much rather have these gorgeous birds around to look at. I can never get enough of looking at these beautiful creatures!" But that was then, and now was now. Elizabeth's eyes were forever robbed of the privilege to see again.

"Charles, can you hand me a plate, darling? Charles?" Elizabeth sat behind the table on the outdoor patio.

"I'm sorry, what...what did you say?"

"I need a plate," Elizabeth repeated.

"Sure, here you are my darling."

"Are you all right, Charles?"

"Yes, no worries," he said as he reached for his wife's hand and kissed the inside of her palm. Annie looked at both of her parents. She simply adored them. She knew, her father had a hard time accepting his wife's unexpected blindness. But she also knew that her mother took the best out of the situation, and that's what she concentrated on, for the sake of her husband. She was the stronger one. She always has been.

Chapter 3

Marco woke up early; he could no longer sleep. The air was unusually warm for spring that year. He looked out of the open window. Bright stars lit the sky while quietness filled the air. Perhaps it was the full moon that didn't let him sleep. His grandfather had always said that the full moon makes people and animals do *weird* things. It can make them go crazy. The cows would go into labor all at once, the chickens would produce a whole lot more eggs, and his father, Walter Wagner, would drink until he fell on the ground and passed out. This was true. Marco still shivered at the memory of the afternoon on the previous day. After his father stumbled and lay in the grass by the pond, Marco ran away. He had seen his father like this many, many times. He knew better to leave him alone. Let him sleep it off. He learned this the hard way. Once, when he reached his hand to help to lift his drunken body up, he didn't realize how strong the alcohol made his father to act.

"Don't need no help from you, you little rat!" yelled Wagner. He spit blood on the kitchen floor from his liquored mouth. Marco still felt he had to help him, so he reached his arm again toward his father, when Wagner grabbed him and put all of his body weight onto Marco's arm. *Snap.* Marco heard his own bone crack under the weight of his father's body. The pain that followed was unbearable. He started crying, and his mother came to the rescue. Just at twelve years old, his own helping hand betrayed him.

"You little wus, you ain't no son of mine!"

No one listened anymore to what the drunk had to say. Marco's mom lifted her son and rushed him out of the house, across the field, around the pond into her father's house. She banged on the wooden door, until her father Vin opened.

"I'm going to kill that bastard!" Marco heard his grandfather's strong voice. Then he passed out.

The twenty-year-old, tall and handsome man, looked back from the mirror at Marco. A strand of curly hair covered his left eye. He brushed his fingers through the dark, thick hair. His eyes shifted to his arm. No one could ever tell it had been broken. The memory was forever imprinted in his mind, yet very distant now. Leaving the window open, Marco returned back to his bed. He worried about his mom, often wishing there was more he could do for her. Isabel meant everything to him. She was a gentle, sweet woman, so pretty and used to be so happy. Isabel made chores look fun and easy, just like the times when she taught him to read and write. She would show him an apple, and then she would put the word "apple" on a piece of paper. His mother would tirelessly spell it for him, over and over again. Isabel had so much patience with him. He knew how to write apple and cow first, before he learned how to spell his own name. The thought created a slight smile on his face while his head was buried in the pillow.

Funny, Marco thought, despite his first Italian name, he will always be Magpie for his beloved grandfather. And he wouldn't want to have it any other way! He heard about the magpie that came and sat on the branch outside of the window when he was born. He heard all about it. Besides, he liked magpies. He sort of identified with them. Their fathers were deep black, in fact so black, that when the sun shined straight through the bird's feathers, one could see shades of blue, and green in them. That's how Marco's own hair was. He will always remain Marco for his mom just as he always would be Magpie for his beloved grandfather. As Marco lay in his bed, he thought what the day may bring to them on that early spring morning, hoping the full moon would be graceful to them; they already had lots on their minds. Aware of his mother's wish to leave Wiley to go study, he hadn't had the guts to tell her, he already made up his mind to become a farmer just like his grandfather. He also couldn't leave the place and have his mother stay alone in the house with that drunk. He thought so hard, and before he knew it, he made himself to fall asleep again.

The full moon sure didn't make their day easier. As expected, Vin Savelli found himself in the barn surrounded by crazy sheep on that early, Tuesday morning. Two sheep had already delivered their babies that were doing fine on their own. But the third sheep, whose baby was standing in the corner of the barn all alone, needed his attention fast. Vin looked at her, and thought to himself that he might not be able to fix the problem himself. When the sheep went into labor, she pushed so hard her insides came out together with her baby sheep. The uterus was hanging outside her rare end, and blood was all around the sheep's back legs, and straw. Even her baby looked like a bloody mess. Vin had seen this before. He had seen in it in both cows and sheep. He knew he needed an extra pair of hands. The old Italian rushed to get his grandson. Time was running out for the newborn baby, who couldn't suck on mother's milk. The mama sheep didn't want the baby nowhere near her. Vin tried to bring the baby to the other sheep, who also delivered on that Tuesday morning, but both of them didn't want to accept the estranged baby. Marco had helped him before, when cow's insides got out. But this was a little bit more difficult. Sheep are smaller and narrower, and to put things back in place are thus much more difficult.

Vin said, "Magpie, come over here, behind the sheep and lift her hind legs in the air and hold them up for me!"

Marco replied, "Okay!" He raised the sheep's legs and Vin quickly grabbed the uterus in his hands, and tried to pushed it back into the sheep's body. The animal, already in a lot of distress, didn't want to cooperate with them. She started turning and twitching. Vin wiped a stream of sweat coming down his temples.

"I think I got it all inside now!" Vin said with exhaustion, as he wiped his sweaty forehead. "Jeez, it's hot today!"

Marco asked, "Do you think she needs to be stitched?"

Vin said with a smile on his face, "Noo, no I don't. She needs to stop pushing, though, when her baby is born, that's what she needs to do!"

"Go to your mamma now, go!" Vin turned the baby sheep toward her mom. The men left the rest to nature. The baby started sucking on mama's milk. That day the farm became richer with three new healthy baby sheep. Marco wiped the bloody sheep's end with a wet cloth, and then he shoveled away the stained bedding and replaced it with fresh straw.

Vin looked down on his messy trousers and shirt. "Now I better go an' clean up!" The old farmer turned his back and walked out of the barn. Farm's life was a tough work, but he wouldn't exchange it for any other in the world. He liked the rewards it brought back in exchange of a day of hard labor. That day's reward came in three healthy and happy lambs. When Marco was a child, he used to name the newborn animals. What would he name these three lambs now? A smile appeared on his face. He moved his hat higher on his head and away from the forehead, whispering toward the lambs, "*Tiny* that would be your name." The smallest lamb didn't pay any attention to him, still sucking on mama's milk.

"You would be *Smudge,* because you have a dark freckle on your nose!" Marco said to the second lamb that was curled up next to his mama's belly. "And you would be named *White Pearl,* because you are the most beautiful of them all! Consider this a blessing, my lambs." He got up and brushed the straw from his pants. Then he walked toward the morning sun and outside of the barn. His empty stomach grouched as he headed back to the house.

Isabel prepared a pot of strong, dark chicory coffee. She he cut a thick slice of homemade rosemary bread and placed the slices in the willow basket.

"Here, the bread is still warm," she said, placing the food in front of her father. Vin took a knife and spread some homemade butter on it. He rolled salami out of the paper and cut several pieces out of it. The butter was a delicious sweet cream that just melted in his mouth. Almost every produce he ate came out of his own stock. He was proud to have the best cream in the whole county. At least he considered it to be the best. He took a sip of the black chicory coffee. Vin's always loved the smell and the taste. The sweet, yet nutty taste stayed present around the Savelli's household. His own mother would drink it from morning until the time, she went to bed. So did his father. Unlike real coffee, chicory didn't have any caffeine in it, so young kids could drink it, too. The Savelli's would start their day by placing a large pot full of water on the wooden stove. When the water went into a boil, Vin's mother added spoons of the chicory mix. Besides the chicory plant, the mix contained sugar beets, barley and rye grains. Another thing he liked about it was, that unlike coffee, this chicory mix tasted good whether it be hot or cold. When Magpie was just three years old, he introduced him to this dark, pot of goodness. At first, his grandson did not like it at all.

The little boy asked, "Why is it so dark, grandpa?"

Vin replied, "Because it's made out of dark grains."

"Are there monsters inside the cup?"

"Monsters? Bahaha!" His grandfather's laugh filled in the small kitchen. Vin reached for a cup of milk. "The milk will chase the black monsters away. Watch." Vin poured the white liquid into the cup. The little boy smiled. And ever since that day, Marco has been drinking chicory coffee with his grandfather. Vin made a sigh when he realized, how many years have passed since. He reached for milk and poured it into the coffee. His cows produced so much of it that people often came to his farm to buy milk and cream from him. They would also buy cheese that his sheep produced. The sheep's milk had certain healing powers; at least that's what the local town people believed. Vin didn't see anything special about the sheep's milk, except, if you had a problem to go to the bathroom, then a cup or two of sour or sweet helped you in an instant! He truly enjoyed every animal he had on his farm. Every single one served its purpose. Besides a source of meat, the cows produced milk, from milk he could make butter, the sheep's milk could be converted into a cheese, plus their wool kept the Savelli's family warm all winter long. The hens produced their eggs every day, and there were so many possibilities to make a single egg go a long way in the kitchen! The pigs were kept alive until they weighted enough, then their body was slaughtered and used almost in its entirety for the food purpose. Vin preferred to use the rifle instead of knife. He never enjoyed bloody field, and didn't like to see the animal suffer. Under all that muscle, deep voice and dark eyes, Vin Savelli had a gentle soul. But only the closest members of his family got to see this softer side of the otherwise tough, old Italian.

Chapter 4

Elizabeth Newman opened her right palm. Annie handed her a brush. She sat down on the edge of bed, next to her mother.

"Your hair is like velvet, mother, so soft and silky."

"Thank you, Annie. Can you see any silver strands there, yet?" Elizabeth's voice signaled she was joking.

Annie smiled, "No, mother. Your hair is beautiful, strawberry blonde, just like mine." Feeling a sudden throb of sadness inside, she looked in the mirror at the reflection of them. The sentiment always brought back the reality check, that her mother in fact, was blind. Annie struggled to accept it fully, even though her mother hadn't been able to see for many years now.

"Annie?"

"Yes, mother?"

"I am glad to hear that." Elizabeth lifted her right hand in the air. Annie instantly reached for her mother's palm. Elizabeth's soft skin and thin long fingers mixed with Annie's hand and became one.

"You are ready to show the world how beautiful you are, dear mother." Annie wrapped her arms around Elizabeth's slim torso and hugged her.

Elizabeth smiled, feeling her warm daughter's cheek leaning on her own. She kissed it and replied, "Let's have a tea outside. It's a beautiful day, and we should enjoy it while it lasts."

The bright sun shined upon the wooden patio attached to the first floor of the house and that overlooked the tall and thick trunks of cottonwood trees that surrounded the property. The large deck faced the south side of the estate, which made it the most suitable to enjoy breakfasts, brunches and late afternoon lunches. Behind those tall, majestic trees lay sparse Montana meadows that continued until they joined the Rocky Mountains at the periphery of their beautiful view.

Elizabeth stirred a spoon of sugar in her warm coffee, "Do you like your horse Annie? Is it a good horse? I tried to pick the best one for you."

Annie held the fine china cup in her hand replied. "Yes mother. Digby is the best horse there is. We rode for hours yesterday. Just hanging out, riding out through the meadows, with no particular reason to get to some place...Just me and my horse, blissfully blessed with all we have."

"I miss those days. I wish I could go for a ride with the two of you." Elizabeth's face broke into a wry smile.

"Oh mother!" Annie reached for her mother's hand, but Elizabeth shied away. "You can sit on the saddle behind me; you know we can still go for a ride together like this."

A bird joined them and started singing his solo for the two ladies. Elizabeth smiled and tilted her head toward the alluring high tone. "Someone's having a good day. The sun feels so good." Elizabeth took of her hat and pointed her face up toward the midday sun.

Annie teased her, "You'll have freckles, mother!"

Elizabeth laughed. They kept quiet for the rest of the lunch. Perhaps they didn't want to interrupt the lovely song that the veery on a nearby branch started singing to them. Elizabeth knew veeries were very shy birds, and the males usually sing at sunset. She felt honored to hear that this male didn't let them wait, and decided to make their lunch brighter with his beautiful song.

⚜

Charles Newman stood on the street looking up at his sign. The downtown street was wide and surrounded by brick buildings on each side. C. E. Newman's bank officially opened for customers a week ago. Charles felt proud he could expand his business to this charming small town. At first he was hesitant whether the move will affect his wife and daughter, but they seem to adjust to their new surroundings fast and without problems. He hoped to bring good business to locals. He smiled, liking the hand-painted sign above the bank's entrance. A few passersby walked on the sidewalk, waving his direction in greeting. Charles lifted his hat and nodded toward them. He picked his own employees and believed in going to work every day, and was always willing to help them if needed. He worked for the future.

✤

"Magpie! I bet you couldn't wait for this day to come." Vin handed a scythe to his grandson. "I already sharpened it." The men stood in the middle of the large grassy field. The stables tickled Marco's bare calves. He placed the scythe in on the ground, and rolled down his trousers. Then he rolled up his white shirt sleeves and moved his hat further over his eyes, to shield against the bright sun. He looked at Vin, who already started cutting the grass on the other hand of the field. He moved fast, swinging his shoulders and hips left to right, left to right, tirelessly into his own rhythm, leaving the freshly cut grass behind his back. Then he suddenly stopped as if he felt Marco's eyes watching him. "What are you waiting for Magpie? Get to work, boy!" Vin's deep voice yelled across the meadow. Marco wrapped his hands firmly around the scythe's wooden handle. He swung from side to side in a fast pace, stopping only to re-sharpen the bottom blade. He felt the drops of sweat on the back of his neck coming down in the middle of his back. The men left the cut grass to dry in the hot Montana sun. They would come back in a day to rake it and turn it on the other side, to make sure it was dry to turn into hay for their farm animals to eat during the winter months.

In the afternoon, Marco collected all the egg from grandpa's hens. He fed the chickens the mixture of grain and old soup that the family didn't finish eating. Then he cut green leaves from the garden and placed them in an iron bucket. The hens and chicken immediately rushed to the iron bucket. Their beaks competed who tore the bigger piece of the green lettuce, a treat they got in exchange for the large eggs they produced. Marco then placed carrots and apple skin into rabbit's cage. They had only two rabbits, and they were more pets than a source of food. They had a spacious cage that Vin built for them in the barn they shared with multiple chickens, hens, one rooster, three sheep and now their recently born three lambs. Vin talked about buying a pig, which Marco was looking forward to. But now, they had to cut the sheep's wool. This type of work wasn't as easy as it may seem. There was a trick to cutting the long and thick wool with a special pair of scissors. Yes, the same scissors they used to cut the curved rooster's nails. One sheep didn't want to be held, and it was twitching and turning to the point, his grandfather got annoyed by the uncooperative sheep that he had to tie its legs together. Marco didn't like to see that. He didn't like to see the animal suffer.

"Grandpa, it looks like it hurts."

"This sheep ain't smart one!" Vin said sharply.

Marco watched his grandfather as his large, thick fingers slid through the large scissor's loops. He then gripped the sheep, that lay on the ground and put her head up high in his lap. He started working from head to tail, and then down on her belly. He worked fast, and the sheep looked as it relaxed more in his lap. There were no cuttings, no blood. Marco learned his technique. They collected the wool into a large back. The nearly naked sheep looked so different. She was now snowy white and resembled her baby lamb. As soon as Vin untied her legs, she quickly rushed to join her baby; her short tail shook from side to side, and she let out a joyful sound. Soon after the sheep number two and three followed. And that was the farmer's life. The Savelli's had three large bags of wool that Vin was ready to bring to the market and sell it.

Another busy day on the farm ended with a stunning sunset. When the Savelli men returned to the house, Isabel served them dinner.

Vin asked his daughter, "Where's your husband?"

Isabel quietly replied, "I don't know where he is. I haven't seen him."

Marco kept quiet. He felt tired, not because of the manual labor, but because of the desperate situation there were in. No matter how hard he tried, he has never found a common speech with his father. He finally gave up; he no longer wanted to understand the reasons *why*.

Vin sliced four thick pieces of his homemade smoked bacon, cut a thick slice of rosemary bread that his daughter baked that morning, and spread a generous amount of butter on it. Then he placed the smoked bacon on top and poured a cup of chicory coffee for his grandson. He watched Magpie adding milk and sugar in the chicory blend and taking a huge bite out of the bacon sandwich. After the men ate, they went to the barn to milk the cows. This repeated every day, twice a day. The cows were milked early in the morning and then again in the evening. Marco placed a fresh stack of hay in the feeder. It kept the cow occupied and it was easier to milk her. Then he placed a clean bucket under her belly. A white, cotton sheet covered the top of the bucket serving as a sieve and keeping all other residue to fall down to milk. He reached for another clean cotton sheet and dipped it in another bucket that had hot water in it. Then he cleaned the cows, before he milked her. They kept the milk in glass jars in a cold dark cellar. Locals often stopped and purchased the Savelli's produce from milk, to sheep cheese to sweat butter cream.

All the work exhausted Marco, but he looked forward to tomorrow. He liked pigs. And tomorrow he'd pick one of his own.

The evening breeze blew over Marco's face as he untied his horse's reins. He jumped into the saddle and rode off into sunset. He stopped far away from the farm. He let his horse drink from the mountain lake, while sat down on a boulder. His eyes couldn't get enough of the beautiful scenery that surrounded him. The sunset came fast, with the last sight of sun on the sky before it went down and behind the mountains. A light, swishing sound drew closer from a left side. Marco turned his head and saw a hare looking back at him. The curious gray wild rabbit stood on his hind legs, sticking his head above the grassy stables, his nose working overtime, and his mouth chewing on something. Marco raised his hand and waved at the hare. As it disappeared into the grass, Marco smiled. A sound of horses' hooves entered the air. Marco got up on his feet. He wasn't expecting a company. This was his place of solitude.

"Digby, slow down!" he heard a young woman's voice shout from the distance. "Hey, slow down, Digby!" The voice came out stronger and louder the second time.

"Digby, slow down, oh my god, you are going to kill us!"

Marco quickly rushed forward in front of the horse, catching his flying rains in the air. It took off all of his power in his arms to stop the horse.

"Ouch, that hurt!" She placed both of her hands on her lower back. Still on the ground, she looked around. Digby stood about twenty feet away from her. She saw a slim figure by his side. She pushed herself up back on her feet.

"Are you okay?" the voice next to her horse yelled at her.

"Yeah, I think so," she yelled back, while trying to see who that person is. The morning sun blinded her eyes. She placed her right hand above her eyebrows. Now, Digby and the person kept walking toward her. She was finally able to see the young man holding onto the Digby's reins. Annie felt relieved.

"Thanks for catching him. We heard a loud bang, and after that he just took off running, and I couldn't get him to stop. Thanks again." The minute she looked into Marco's eyes, she also felt the rush of her own blood entering every single vein in her cheeks. She blushed as she bit her lower lip.

"What's your horse's name?" Marco asked without shifting his eyes from hers.

"Digby."

"That's a nice name for a pretty horse like this."

"Thank you. You saved us." She pushed her slim body up on the horse's back.

Marco looked up at the young girl in the saddle. She smiled at him, and he smiled back at her. "I'm Annie," she said.

⚜

The sound of broken plates woke him up. His heart raced. He heard his parents argue downstairs. What time was it? He looked toward the window. The sky was dark, and overcast. There were no stars, no moon he could see. His father was drunk. A part of him wanted to go downstairs and protect his mother. The other part kept telling him, to stay in bed. He battled his own private struggle. He'd heard his parents argue before, but this time something was telling him *this is going to be different*. Something else flew across the room and broke, followed by pieces of furniture. Marco jumped out of bed. He no longer paid attention to his inner voice that kept telling him to stay away. He opened a window and stepped onto the roof, and then he paused for a second, before he turned his body toward the ground. He jumped. Barefooted and just wearing his underwear, he ran as fast as he could. The rain beat hard on him, and he fought the strong wind in his face. He passed the pond; there were no birds there at this night hour, and then he passed the pastures, where the cows had a feast the previous day. When he got to his grandfather's house, he banged on his door, until Vin's light from the kerosene lamp came up.

"It's mom," he said catching his breath. His tears rolled down his cheeks, and his entire body shook. Vin grabbed a shovel that leaned on the side of his house, and they both rushed back to Marco's house. He found himself in a horrible nightmare, surrounded by darkness and demon voice that were too familiar to him. The demon was inside his house and had his mother's life in its hands. Marco watched his grandfather, as he quietly entered the house, carrying the shovel in his right hand.

"It's for the protection," he whispered toward Marco's shaking shadow. Vin placed his thick index finger over his own mouth. Marco felt his head move up and down, in agreement, but no words came out of his mouth. Once inside, Vin carefully watched every step he took. There was broken glass, plates, chairs scattered all around the kitchen's wooden floor. Then he saw what he has feared the most. There, behind the flipped dining table, laid his daughter's body on the floor. On the top of her was her drunken husband. She was desperately gasping for air, coughing. Her eyes rolling and her face red and swollen. Wagner's hands jiggled violently and had a firm grip around Isabel's neck. Vin saw his daughter dying right in front of his eyes. He tried to keep himself calm, without making any noise. He had to act now, in order to save his only daughter's life. He quietly stepped right behind the drunken man's feet, lifted the shovel in the air, and executed one, strong and very precise strike into the demon's head! Wagner's body instantly fell over Isabel's lifeless flesh. Vin threw the shovel away, then he kicked the demon's body and it rolled onto the floor. The old Italian knelt down and checked for the pulse on Isabel's neck.

"Thank God!" he said gratefully. "Wake up, Bella, wake up." He shook her limp body. "It's over. He'll never hurt you again! It's over now!" But Isabel just laid there motionless. He placed his ear over her chest. He didn't hear any heartbeat. He immediately opened her mouth, and placed his large hands over her slim chest.

"One, two, three, four, five!" he counted out load, while pressing down her chest. Then he exhaled air into her mouth. Vin repeated it over and over again, until he heard his daughter's gasped for air, then she started coughing.

"Oh, thank God, you're back, my Bella!" Vin broke down crying. He hugged his daughter, and then he kissed her forehead.

"Where is he?" she whispered, struggling to get the words out of her throat.

"Gone."

Isabel held her right hand over her neck. Tears rolled down her swollen cheeks.

"Dad..." She had bloody eyes; the choking caused the little blood vessels in them to rupture. Isabel had the demon's imprinted fingers in her neck. But she was alive. She asked quietly, "Where is Marco?"

Magpie! Vin completely forgot about his grandson. Did he run back to his house or was he still waiting outside? He got up and went to the door, checked the outside, but didn't see him there. Then he turned to his daughter and answered her question. "He is safe. He is at my house." He kicked the shovel out of the way so Isabel wouldn't see it. He helped her to get up from the floor. He handed her a towel, and she went to the sink and splashed her face with cold water. She looked down at her trembling hands.

"Here. Sit down." Vin lifted the only chair, that wasn't broken off of the floor and placed it for Isabel to sit down. Then the horror of the night fully dawned on her, and she started uncontrollably shaking. Vin moved the second chair, whose back was broken, and sat down next to his daughter. He held her hand and the two sat there accompanied by silence.

"Everything's goin' to be okay," he said finally. "He ain't gonna hurt you again."

✦

Marco couldn't move from the time, his grandfather left him outside the house in the dark. He was supposed to run back to Vin's, but his feet became heavy and glued to the ground. He was afraid to breathe, thinking he would make too much noise and drag attention to himself. The moment was so surreal. His head facing the kitchen window, his eyes watching everything that was happening. He screamed in his head, he didn't want to see it, but there was nothing he could do. He wasn't in charge of his own body anymore. He saw his grandfather inside the kitchen. He saw the shovel in his hand. Then he watched, as his grandfather suddenly stopped. After a few seconds, all he saw was the shovel being raised in the air. He recognized the thick, farmer's hand and fingers. The rest happened so fast. The shovel went up and down through the air only one time. Marco then heard the metal bounced from the wooden floor inside the kitchen. His instinct made him to cover his eyes. *Nooo,* the inner voice screamed in his head. He started running, his bare feet burring in the ground, on the little rocks, and then over the grass, he ran as fast as he could, his feet slipping in the deep mud, the heavy rain caused. Tears came down his cheeks; he didn't stop until he got to his grandfather's house. There, inside the room, his body collapsed.

Chapter 5

"Good morning my sunshine!" Isabel greeted her son. She stood in the kitchen, making scrambled eggs with bacon. Next to the pan was a freshly brewed chicory coffee. The kitchen's inviting smell made Marco's stomach growl.

"Did you sleep well, Magpie?" his grandfather asked.

At first, Marco didn't know whether this was a part of his dream. He did have a very strange dream last night. He couldn't remember what it was; he just knew, the dream was scary and almost unreal. He looked at his mother fist, and then he looked at his grandfather. "Good morning," he said quietly, studying their faces. Why would he do that? What made him to pay extra attention what his mother looked like on that summer morning? His stomach growled again, this time the sound was louder and noticeable to others.

"You're hungry! That's always a good sign Magpie!" Vin's face showed a delighted smile.

"Sit down, I'll pour you a cup of coffee," his mother said to him. "The food will take only a few more minutes."

Marco joined his grandfather at the table. There was something very odd about that morning. He just couldn't figure out what it was. His mother was making breakfast, while his grandfather sipped his chicory coffee. Their grandfather visited them often in the morning, especially if it was on the weekend.

The fact that Marco's father wasn't present didn't surprise him. Marco's father was often asleep, still hung over from the heavy drinking from the previous night. Thus Marco assumed his father is either upstairs in his bedroom or outside asleep in the field.

"Here you are." Isabel placed a hot mug with chicory coffee in front of Marco. The sweet smell of the blend made his mouth water. He reached for a small jar of milk and poured generous amount into the dark blend. He watched as the dark color mixed with the white milk. Then he put three spoonfuls of sugar into the mug stirring it with a spoon. He slowly sipped the coffee.

Isabel placed the plates in front of her two favorite people in the world. Then she grabbed another plate for herself and joined them behind the table. They ate their eggs with bacon without saying a word.

The nightmare was on Marco's mind. It absorbed his entire brain. He asked, "Isn't father going to join us for breakfast?"

Vin quickly replied back, "No."

"No, he won't join us this morning. Eat your breakfast, Marco. And don't you worry none." Isabel spoke with a quiet, calm voice. She wore a long sleeve dress and a scarf around her neck. She explained she came down with cold. Marco didn't believe her.

Later that day, the two horses made rattle with halter chains and their hooves stirring the dirt underneath their feet formed clouds of dust in the air. Marco waited for his grandfather to step in the carriage. The familiar sound of the snapping reins swished through the air.

"Heya!" Marco yelled loudly, and the horses moved forward. They headed to town to buy a pig and sell some cheese and butter. They were the only travelers on the Montana road. Vin kept quiet, and the only sound were the clopping horses hooves leaving a cloud of dust behind them. Marco's mind shifted to Annie, the girl he met the day before. She told him her father moved to town to open his new bank. She spoke with a soft, educated voice. Marco almost felt simple next to her. Annie used words that could only be found in one of those books that Marco had never read. Yet, she smiled at him often when she spoke. Marco looked ahead on the road. The only signs after last stormy night were the large peddles of muddy water. The market in town had always drawn a crowd of locals. Vin was a good seller and always sold out fast. People trusted him and liked his produce. The customers would return buying more of his sheep cheese, fresh eggs or sweet cream butter. Marco looked around if he's going to see Annie or his father. He hoped to the girl, as much as he hoped not to see the latter. But his eyes went through the crowed several times, mapping the faces around him, his ears listening to different voices, but none belonged to Annie or Walter Wagner. When Vin sold the last bar of butter, they moved over to the livestock. Marco let the way to the pig section. There, they were several fenced lots, each containing smaller and larger pigs inside. Marco came closer to the wooden fence. He kneeled down and slid his arm through the fence. The smallest pig picked up on Marco's hand smell. The little pink piglet came closer and started nibbling on Vin's fingers.

Vin pointed his thick index finger on the limping pig. "This one."

"Are you sure?" The owner couldn't hide his surprise. "The pig has a limp, looks like the runt of the litter."

"Yeah. I'm sure."

Marco picked up the little piglet, which was not more than three months old. He was the smallest one, and one of his legs was shorter than the others, causing him to walk funny, always leaning more on one side, than the other. He had a black spot in the middle of his back.

"Spot," Marco said out loud.

"What?" the man who sold the pig asked.

"That's his name. Spot," Marco repeated.

"Whatever." The man didn't care. What he cared was the money he got paid for the runt piglet. "If you didn't pick him I was ready to sell him to slaughter. I dunno who would want him." The man laughed as Marco and Vin and Spot exited the market. On the way back to the horse carriage Vin waved at a woman. She was a small statue, skinny and dressed in a very expensive dress. Her overly large hat covered most of her face. She waved back at Vin and her face broke into a delighted smile. Then her eyes shifted to Marco. He knew her name was Trudy Webb. She was a wealthy widow, who owned a large house downtown Wiley, two streets from the market. Why did she greet his grandfather? What could possibly the two have in common? Trudy gave Marco a long look. He felt her eyes mapping him from head to toe. His lips said hello, although no voice came out of his mouth. Trudy Webb rewarded him with a wide smile. Then the old, skinny woman disappeared in the middle of the crowd.

Marco spent the rest of the day outside. He put Spot on a lead made out of rope and walked with him to the pond. The pig's limp didn't slow him down. He introduced all the ducks and other wild birds to Spot, and the little piglet happily wiggled its tale around. Some people had dogs, Marco had a pig. He used to have a dog. When it died, probably of old age, Marco cried for a month.

The clouds came up on the Montana sky and covered the sun. Soon after, the first rain drops came down on his raven curly hair. He got up, pick up Spot into his arms and rushed back to the house. The prevalent feeling the events of last night weren't just his nightmare stayed with him for the rest of the day. His father never came home. He didn't join them for dinner. Yet Isabel insisted nothing happened. Marco knew his father often stayed out for days. When he drank his money out, he would show up at the house, begging for more, and everything would repeat.

"Where's that chair, mother?" he asked after they finished eating.

"What?"

"The fourth chair is missing." Marco tilted his head to the empty spot behind the table.

"Oh. That chair! One of the legs got loose, so I took it out for your grandfather to fix it."

Marco didn't believe a word his mother said. "Aren't you hot wearing a long sleeve and a scarf around your neck?"

"What?" Isabel looked at her son. "Why do you have so many questions, son?"

"I just think it's too hot to wear a long sleeve and a scarf around. That's all."

Isabel quickly got up and walked away from the table. Marco watched her, as she placed the dirty dishes into a sink.

"I told you, I've got cold," said Isabel. She nervously loosened up her scarf.

"I met a girl the other night. Her name is Annie Newman. Her father is a banker."

"A girl? That's great, Marco. Why don't you bring her over for a coffee and cake tomorrow? I'd like to meet her."

"Will father be here, too?"

"No. I...I don't know.

"Here, go sit down. I'll wash the dishes." Marco kissed his mother's cheek.

Are you gonna lay down your lie? Wagner's voice whispered in Isabel's head. She shivered and walked out of the kitchen door.

✦

"Grandpa? Paps?" Marco looked around. He went from the kitchen into the living room, then he entered Vin's only bedroom. The house was empty. Marco used the side door to go out and look for him. Maybe he went into the barn, and decided to feed the animals early, Marco thought. Rain poured hard again. He ran from the house, across the yard and into the barn. "Grandpa, are you here?" Marco walked through the barn, looking around, but all he saw were the farm animals. "Where are you?" he muttered under his lips.

Marco was about to turn back to go to Vin's house when his legs stumbled onto something hard and sharp. He looked down at the hay stack. With his foot, he spread the hay around, and there he saw it! Marco's body started shaking; he felt his stomach up his throat. The young farmer's head spun, and his worst nightmare just became a reality. Down, on the ground covered by the hay, laid the bloody shovel. The events of last night immediately flooded Marco's mind. What he thought was just a nightmare, proved to be a real thing. The bloody tip of the shovel stared back at him. A few straws of hay were glued in the dried blood. His father wasn't coming back, ever again. Strangely, Marco felt a sense of relief. Then he felt guilty for not feeling any sorrow. Was he supposed to be sad? Will he miss his father? Where was his grandfather? And where is his father's body?

"Oh no!" he whispered. He covered the shovel with hay, then he ran out of the barn. He stopped in the middle of the field turning around and making sure he was alone. Then he screamed out loud before falling down to his knees and crashing into the tall grass. Everything made sense to him now. His mother wore long-sleeved dress and had a scarf on her neck this morning at breakfast because she didn't want him to see the bruises on her neck. But did she know? Was Isabel aware Walter Wagner was forever gone? Grandfather moved two chairs from his house into his daughter's house, before Marco got up for breakfast. Just a few hours ago, his father was drunk and furious like never before. Marco remembered he ran for help to grandpa's house. Then he remembered his grandfather had ordered him to return to his house and stay inside. But Marco couldn't move. The next thing he remembered was seeing his grandfather inside the kitchen and the shovel in his hand. All it took was one strong stroke. He didn't remember running back to grandpa's house. He didn't know how he got back to his own bed. What he knew and what he was sure about was that his grandfather saved his mother's life last night. Then he realized what he had witnessed, only three people know about — his grandfather, his mother, and himself. Or was he wrong? He didn't see his mother last night or she was on the floor and his father was lying on the top of her motionless body...Could it be, that his mother didn't see what happened to her drunken husband last night? That would make Marco the one and only witness, and his grandfather the only suspect. This would make only two people in the whole of Montana who knew what happened to the drunk. One, who had to protect his daughter to save her life, and the other who had to protect them both. Self-doubt suddenly washed over him. Would he be able to keep it a secret? Would he be able to protect his mother and his grandfather? There were only two people in the whole entire world that meant the most to him. He couldn't bear the thought loosing either of them. This was his duty, to keep the events that unfolded on that spring night of 1925, a secret. Marco made a promise to himself. He swore, he will never let his grandfather know, what he had witnessed. Then he swore to again, he would protect his grandfather no matter the circumstance or cost. He knew that what his grandfather did was an act of love. He made Isabel and him free of the demon's trap. But where was Walter Wagner's body?

✦

What a day! Marco sighed as he slipped under the blanket. He felt beat up, even though he really didn't do much that day. Yet, he uncovered something huge, something he would never forget until the day he died: He thought he did pretty well considering what the day brought to him.

After he came upon the bloody shovel in the barn, he ran back to his mother's house. He looked for clues, but then he decided his mother didn't know anything. She was looking for her husband's whereabouts by lunch time. When she didn't find him anywhere near house, she asked Marco, whether he had seen his father. Marco told her he hadn't seen him, which wasn't a lie. When Isabel asked Vin where her husband may be, Marco quietly studied his grandfather's face. He hoped he would see something, a clue, some glitch, some body language that would make him confirm his darkest thoughts. But there was nothing unusual in Vin's face or his answer.

"No, I haven't seen him. For what I know, he's probably still asleep somewhere in the fields. Wouldn't be the first time!"

But what did his grandfather do with his body? If he hit his drunken father with a shovel, then how did he manage to drag him out of the house and where exactly would he put him? How had his mother not seen anything? Or had she? Was this some kind of a game they were playing with Marco? For God's sake, all these questions and no answers! What if his father was not dead? What if he is coming back to get them? No, it can't be. He must be dead. There was blood on the shovel. No matter what, he was sure, this happened for a reason. *What am I going to do, I have to protect my grandfather, that's the only thing I know I have to do. Will I be able to keep it a secret? I can't keep secrets. I have never been able to keep anything from my grandfather. Should I tell him that I know what I saw? What I saw him to do? Oh, God, help me with this. And how am I supposed to look at my mom, when I know, when I know...what I saw? Maybe I should go and tell grandpa, maybe I will feel better. I will tell him I know what he did and that it is okay with me. That he did what he had to do, to protect me and mom.*

Chapter 6

PERSONA

I am with you when you wake up,
I am with you at the end of the day.
I can make you feel happy,
I can make you feel sad.
I am your Persona.
I am your friend, but I can be your enemy.
I am your character,
But I am not whole.
I am what others see in you,
Yet you know there is more.

You took on a face and a voice,
But was it all in your choice?
You know better who you are.

You act strong and confident,
But only I know, when we are alone
You change and moan.

And I've thrown this in your face
Yet you still need to chase for what is your own
So don't be afraid, go and embrace –
You know you always have to walk alone.

Chapter 7

She met him at the mountain lake, by the large boulder. Their bodies united, and their lips locked against one another. The sun shined up high in the sky, and the warm breeze moved Annie's hair away from her face. She loved the smell of summer. The air smelled like an Indian paintbrush with the sweet and gentle fragrance of the prairie-fire colored plant that spread across the meadow. The colors varied from bright red to shades of orange and yellow, and the plant stood straight up against the sky.

They spent hours by the lake, hidden in the valley of the Rocky Mountains, sometimes riding horses, other times just lying in the grass or cooling down in the cold water of the Hidden Lake. Their bodies blended with the nature, and become one. For the past week and a half they lived their dream, except Marco couldn't confine in her love. Annie asked about his father. The gossip in the small Wiley town spread out fast and caught the interest of the local sheriff McGinnis. She didn't want to think about it. Instead, she let her mind relive her favorite moments she's shared with Marco and one that she wished never existed.

"I'm Marco."

"Annie."

"Nice to meet you, Annie."

"Do you know it well around here?" she asked.

"Yes. I know every branch and every rock there is." he said as he spread his arms wide. "Why?"

"What's your most favorite place?"

Marco hesitated at first. The most favorite place on Earth was the one by the pond, on his grandfather's property.

"Don't you have one?" she insisted.

He shrugged. Why would he share where his favorite place is with some girl, that he just met? She was beautiful, there was no doubt about it. There was something very inviting about her, he thought, she has this light around her, above her...

Her soft spoken voice broke his silence. "I see, you don't want to tell me."

"No, yes, I mean yes, I do want to tell you."

Her smile uncovered a perfect row of white teeth. Then he noticed her dimples. The girl had two cute dimples on each of her cherry-colored cheeks.

"How about now?" She asked as her hazel eyes once again met with his.

It was his turn to smile. He nodded with his head. "Okay, let's go now."

"Perfect," she said as mounting the horse. "Come and join me. All you have to do is to tell Digby where we are going."

And so they slowly let Annie's horse to take them, to Marco's most favorite place in the whole entire Montana. They crossed the wide meadow. Marco kept pointing down at various wildflowers.

"This is called Scarlet Paintbrush," he said as they passed the pinky red flower. Its tip opened just like a brush, with several smaller flowers, on each side of the long, green stem.

"Scarlett Paintbrush." Annie repeated. Summer wildflowers have taken over this wide, mountain meadow.

"This is a Blue Harebell." He pointed at the little flower in the shape of bells. "And the white flowers with the yellow center are..."

Annie jumped in. "Daisies!"

"Right, those are daisies."

"And these are sunflowers," Marco said.

"Of course, I recognize those!" Annie let out a loud smile. She didn't know much about the flora, but she was happily surprised Marco did and he could teach her more.

"Which one is your favorite?" she asked him. Her body moved slightly back, and her forehead lightly brushed over Marco's chin.

Marco made the horse stop. He jumped down and Annie watched him to walk away. He bent down and tore out a single, long stemmed flower. He brought it back to Annie.

"This is a White Rein Orchid. This is my favorite wildflower." He extended his arm to Annie, and she picked up the flower. She almost immediately smelled the fragrant white petals.

"Rein orchid," she whispered. Marco got up on the horse behind her. Annie placed the long stemmed flower behind her cleavage. The tip of the white petals touched her nose and tickled her. She sneezed.

"Bless you," Marco said with a smile on his face.

"Thanks," she said as the smell of the orchid made its way to her nose.

They arrived at the pond. Digby welcomed the fresh, cold water. Then, they tied him up under the large tree, where the shade protected him from the sun. Annie sat down on the grass.

"It's truly beautiful around here," she said. "I can see why this is your most favorite place." The pond was quite large, there were tall trees on one side, and the other side was open, offering a spectacular view of the Rocky Mountains. There was no one else there, except them. She didn't see any houses or people. They were surrounded by nature and the beauty around spoke for itself. She could definitely understand, why this was Marco's favorite place. She felt special that he took her there. They sat there quietly for a moment. They watched the pair of swans as they landed on the pond ahead of them. They watched the swans feeding on the pond under water plants and small fish.

"They are so majestic, with their long necks and wide, snowy white wings. I wonder where did they fly from and where they are heading next." Annie broke off the silence.

"They flew in from the south as they will be heading back there in the fall."

"My mom likes birds, she knows so much about them, just like you."

"Oh no, I don't know much. Just some stuff here, and there. You know, just the things my grandfather told me." Marco looked at her.

Annie shrugged when she heard him say the word grandfather. She was well aware what the town locals were gossiping about. To Annie, those were just gossips, nothing else. "I've heard the rumors people say about your grandfather." She looked directly at Marco's face. He didn't move at all. "I want you to know, I don't believe any of it."

Marco's head tilted down, and then back up.

"Marco?" Annie wasn't sure it was a good idea to shift the talk to his grandfather.

"I guess people have nothing better to do in this small town." Marco broke of a piece of grass and stuck it in his mouth. He started chewing on it. Annie took the rein orchid out of her cleavage and smelled it. "What have you heard?" Marco asked causally, not knowing what to expect for Annie's answer.

"I...they say, that...that your grandfather has something to do with the disappearance of your father," she said with a quiet voice. "I wish there was something I could do."

"My grandfather didn't do anything wrong. He did nothing. I want you to know that." They sat there quietly for a moment, watching the two swans on the pond. The sun was almost in the middle of the sky, as this meant midday was approaching. Marco felt his stomach growl. "Annie, would you like to have some lunch with me today?"

"You mean now?"

"Yes. Now. Me and you. And Digby, of course."

She smiled. "Of course."

"Come. My house is just a few minutes away from here." He helped her to get back on the horse, and then he joined her on Digby's strong back. He navigated the horse to his house.

✤

"Nice to meet you, Annie." Isabel shook hands with Marco's friend. She didn't expect a guest for lunch, but she always made plenty of food, and she was glad to share it with Annie. She welcomed the young girl into her house, and then seated her behind her kitchen table. She kept looking at her son and wondering how fast he had grown up. This was his first time he brought someone home with him. And a girl...a very pretty young lady, at that. Isabel noticed the horse they came on.

She could tell the horse was one of those expensive kinds that only people with serious money could afford to buy. And so she wondered, while serving lunch who this young girl may be, and if the friendship could be genuine. After she placed all the food on the table, she joined them behind the square, wooden desk.

She knew, her father Vin went down to town, and therefore will not be having lunch with them.

Isabel noticed the girl was shy, and rather quiet. She wondered whether she has heard anything about their family. She was almost sure, she must have.

"Annie, is your family knew to town?" Isabel asked her, when they got done eating lunch.

"Yes, well, it depends. My father owns a bank in downtown Wiley."

"Oh, is it the C. E. Newman's bank?"

"Yes madam, it is my father's bank."

"It's nice to see people like your father. We need more men like him, to give jobs to those who need them." Isabel smiled at Annie. She couldn't wait to ask her son how he met her.

"Thank you for lunch, Mrs. Savelli."

Marco showed her the entire farm. He took her down to the stable, where she met with Tuffy. He told her about the horse's injured foot, and that it has been healing nicely. Then he took her to meet the other farm animals. And so Annie met with Milly the calf, and the three lambs, Tiny, Smudge and White Pearl.

"Can I see you again tomorrow?"

"It depends."

"It depends on what?" Marco asked.

Annie hopped on her horse and gave Digby a signal to leave. As the horse started running away, she turned and waived at Marco. He waved back. He met the prettiest girl in the entire whole Montana that day. Her name was Annie Newman.

✦

Annie woke up and looked out of the window. The sky was lit with so many bright stars. Some were smaller, some bigger, some had bright yellow color, while others were lit red and orange. Some stars look as if they were moving and some were flicking on the sky, like a candle in the air. Annie liked looking at the sky. She always found the endless sky both, entertaining and mysterious. Whether the sky was lit with stars, or covered with clouds, and the moon was hiding behind them, she tried to imagine what's behind the clouds. Is there anything at all? Now, the sky had several small clouds that were spread across. One cloud looked like a large snowy mountain while the other two looked like human faces. She could see a nose, mouth and even eyes. Maybe it was her grandmother, up there, in the cloud, smiling at her now. Annie was just one year old, when her granny died. She was her mother Elizabeth's mother. Ever since she was a little girl, her mom told her she got her granny's blonde curly hair and big hazel eyes. Annie idealized her grandmother and liked to look at her old pictures. Margaret Miller was a noble woman who had a sharp mind and witty mouth, her mom always said. She wore a silver brooch in her hair every single day, until the day she died. And then even after her death, Margaret was buried with her bronze in her hair, according to her last wish. She had a mind of her own, just like Annie, her mom would tell her. Annie's middle name was Margaret, and she liked to use it when she made her mom mad.

"Oh, you are so stubborn sometimes!"

"My name is Annie Margaret; I have a reason to be stubborn!" Annie would reply. But all that was in a good humor. Annie rarely had any fights with her mother Elizabeth. They were more like friends, and sisters with each other. Now, looking at the sky, Annie could see the cloud's face change its shape. Definitely, Margaret was watching her from the above. And she still had her silver brochure in her hair. The cloud couldn't hide the silver pin in the sky. Annie recognized it from the many photographs' her mother gave her.

"This is your granny Margaret." Elizabeth placed the wooden box with granny Margaret's photograph's on Annie's bed. Then she opened the hand carved box and took the first photograph out.

"See, you have your granny's eyes and her blonde curly hair."

"Why did she die, Mommy?"

"She was old, that's why. She lived a long, good life. It was her time. But don't worry, granny is still with us. She is in the butterfly you see outside, or she can be the bird, that sat on the branch and watched you eat breakfast." Elizabeth stroked Annie's hair. "That's strange." Annie's face frowned. She couldn't wait for the morning to come.

Chapter 8

Marco's day started with a morning walk with Spot. The little piglet enjoyed walking in the grass. He maneuvered himself pretty well, despite his limp. The little piglet licked dew on the grass and wiggled his tail. The outdoor temperature was brisk, but the sun already made its way up in the sky.

"This is going to be another hot, sunny day. And I'm glad I will enjoy it with you." Marco said to his piglet. They walked out in the field that was surrounded by the majestic Rocky Mountains. "This is the best place on Earth." Marco told Spot.

The piglet's mouth chew on the grass and his nose sniffed around.

"I will take you to the river today. It's my second most favorite place. The first is right here, where we live." Marco looked around. The mountain range in front of him spread as far as his eyes could see. There was a little bit of snow on some of the highest peaks. Then there were bare rocks, and down below was the forest. Marco and Spot were surrounded by the most beautiful nature around. He closed his eyes. The tall grass rustled under the wind. The air ever so crisp, smelled like freshly watered wild flowers. Spot snorted, and Marco opened his eyes. "What? You want to go back?" He spoke to his four-legged friend. "Okay, let's go eat some breakfast."

On his way back from the morning walk, he saw an unfamiliar car parked in front of his mother's house. He suddenly felt a sharp pain in his stomach. He had an idea what it was about. He tied up Spot around a metal post outside of the house. Then his mother came out and waved at him.

"Marco, come here, there is something we have to tell you, dear!" Isabel said loudly. When he entered, he saw his mother and his grandfather Vin sitting behind the table together with Sheriff McGinnis.

"Come sit down with us, Magpie!" his grandfather ordered with his deep voice. Marco hesitantly walked to the table.

Sheriff looked at him directly. "I'm afraid we have some bad news for you, boy."

Marco noticed the man was sweating profusely under his grey suit. His stomach was large, and he had a double chin. *Probably that's why he was sweating so much.* Marco's eyes widened, and he nervously brushed his hand through his curly hair. Sheriff McGinnis spoke first.

"There seems to be a complaint from a local person in town regarding your husband, Mrs. Savelli. Apparently, there was a fight last night in town, in the pub. According to some witnesses, your husband started the fight, and then all the hell broke loose. He hit a man in his head. There was a lot of blood..." Sheriff McGinnis shook his head and then paused for a moment. No one else said a word. "The man survived and gave me the description of the person who attacked him. The description fits your husband. Can I speak to him now?" Sheriff McGinnis looked at Isabel, and then he shifted his eyes toward Vin. Marco didn't know what to do. Questions flooded his mind. He tried his best to keep himself content and not to let anyone know, about his little secret.

"Oh my God, that's terrible!" Isabel gasped in disbelief. She covered her mouth with her hand, and looked over at Vin.

"We haven't seen him. I don't know where the drunk is. She knows nothin'!" Vin canted his head toward his daughter.

The sheriff then looked at Marco. "What about you, young boy, do you know where your father is?"

"He knows nothing," Vin answered sharply.

"Well, then, he can tell me that himself, right boy?" The sheriff's restless eyes looked at Marco's face.

"I don't know where my father might me. I haven't seen him for a while."

"Haven't seen him for a while?" The sheriff repeated without leaving his eyes from Marco.

"Is there anything else, we can do for you today, sheriff?" Isabel got up and expected the same from the authority at his house. "Can I walk you out?"

"No, that won't be necessary." McGinnis finally got up; he placed his hat back onto his sweaty head. Before he exited, he turned around and said angrily, "I will be back, you can count on it."

"We'll look forward to it sheriff, *you* can count on it," Vin replied with a smirk on his face.

All three waited until they no longer could hear the car's rumbling engine. Then Isabel spoke first. "Father, what are we going to do? He could have killed that man...What if he shows up here, drunk again, what are we going to do?"

Marco looked at his grandfather's face. *What are we going to do, if he shows up here, Grandpa? I saw what you did. I will never tell anyone.*

"Marco, are you okay?" Isabel suddenly worried about the look she saw on her son's face.

"Yeah."

"Are you okay – you look so pale? You know, everything will be all right. The men were drunk, both of them, they weren't thinking clearly. I'm sure your father will come home soon. He will have to apologize; maybe he will finally learn his lesson and things will be for the better." "Enough of this talk. I'm starved, aren't you two?" Vin said, changing the subject. But it stayed in the air, as they ate breakfast. Marco peeled an apple and brought it out to Spot. The piglet quickly chewed on the juicy piece of fruit. Marco kept busy for the rest of the day. There was so much work to do around the animals, and in their presence he didn't have time to flood his mind with unanswered questions. Life didn't stop at the farm. The best thing to do was to keep busy. On that sunny summer day, Marco helped to wash Taffy. The old horse appreciated the cold stream of water and the touch of brush. Then he got some carrots and sliced apples to make his day even brighter. The warm sun dried his skin, while he fed on grass on an open pasture. Marco's little helper Spot ran with him while Marco let the cows outside to a fenced area. The piglet maneuvered himself among the cow's feet, like a herding dog. It was a beautiful site that made Marco laugh. This was his first laugh, he realized. *Everything will be all right,* his grandfather's words echoed in his ears. *Everything.*

✦

Sheriff McGinnis shook Charles' hand. "I really appreciate what you have done for us, for our town, and local people who found new jobs at your bank, Mr. Newman."

"Thank you for your kind words, Sheriff. Please, have a seat."

McGinnis looked around Charles' office before he sat down.

"What may I do for you today, Sheriff?"

"I came here today to talk to you about the investigation regarding the disappearance of Walter Wagner."

"You want to talk to me? About the farmer's family?"

"Yes, exactly. You see, I know your daughter is spending a lot of time with the young Savelli boy. Not that this is my business, but—"

Charles Newman frowned and quickly interrupted McGinnis, "No, it's none of your business, Sheriff."

"As I said, there is a pending investigation in the disappearance of the family member. It would be a good idea to keep your daughter away from Marco Savelli at least for some time, until we gather more information."

"Keep Annie away? Is the young boy that much danger?"

"His father disappeared from the surface of the earth basically overnight. You tell me, Mr. Newman, in who's best interest could it be to eliminate Walter Wagner?" The sheriff's eyes looked directly into Charles. "If you feel like you can help, give me a call." The sheriff reached into his grey vest's pocket and took out his business card. "Call me anytime."

Charles put the card into his drawer. Could there possibly be something dangerous, dark and uncalled for from the Savelli's family? Or was just Sheriff McGinnis making things bigger than they really are. But then where was Walter Wagner? Charles decided to look further into this mysterious man, who knew nothing about.

He got up from his wooden desk and walked out into the main lobby. He told his secretary he would be out for the rest of the day. Then he jumped into his car and drove off. He rolled his windows down and let the warm air brush through his hair. He stopped in front of the local bar, not far away from his bank. The inside of the bar was a lot darker than he expected. He sat down and ordered a cold beer.

The baldheaded, short and bulky bartender asked, "How's your day going, Sir?"

Charles took a long sip of the golden colored liquid. "Did you know Walter Wagner?"

The baldheaded short and bulky bartender stopped wiping the surface of the bar with a damp cloth. "Are you a cop?"

Charles wiped the foam from his upper lip and looked directly at the bartender, "No. I'm not a cop. I'm just curious. Did the locals like him? Did he have friends?"

"Wagner!" the bartender said sharply. "Wagner never had any friends. Ever. When he came over here, he would sit by himself. He was a drunk. That's all there is to it. He probably stumbled into a swamp. A dog would not bark after him."

Charles quickly finished his beer, paid the bartender, and walked out. He kept on driving on the only road that led out of town and to the Savelli's farm.

An old horse rested his foot, bent at a knee, and nibbled on hay. Charles immediately thought of his daughter Annie. She would have liked this horse. Had she seen it, has she been to Savelli's farm, he wondered. Then he heard the sheep in the background and saw several chickens eating on the green leaves hanging over a large pot. He stopped the car and walked to the house.

What am I going say, he thought to himself, why am I even here? He was about to turn around and walk away when the door opened.

"Can I help you?"

"Good afternoon, ma'am. My name is Charles Newman." His eyes stared at the thin woman in front of him. She had large brown eyes and long dark, curly hair. She looked frightened. "I...I came to introduce myself. I am a businessman and I have recently opened a bank in downtown Wiley..."

"Yes. I've heard about the new bank in town."

"I'm sorry, I missed your name, ma'am."

"Isabel. I think you came here to speak with my son Marco."

"Pardon me?"

"You didn't come here to introduce your business, Mr. Newman. You came to see who your daughter has been hanging out with. Would you like to come in? I was just about to get some lunch."

Charles heard his grouchy stomach. Lunch was exactly what he needed. He didn't want to intrude himself in like this, but the hunger took over. Charles hesitantly stepped forward and closed the entranced door behind him. He looked around. The dining area and the kitchen were connected, and the interior space was a lot smaller than he expected it to be by looking at the house from the outside. Every piece of furniture had its own space and purpose. He thought of his beloved wife, Elizabeth. She would have a hard time moving around a kitchen and dining area like this. He was so used to living with a blind person that he suddenly found himself feeling uneasy in a place where there were sharp edges, with too many stools and benches around.

"Is there something wrong, Mr. Newman?" Isabel's voice brought him back from his deep thoughts.

"No, no ma'am," he quickly replied and smiled at her. Charles sat and placed both of his hands on the top of the wooden table. There was no tablecloth. He couldn't even remember when was the last time he sat behind a dining table that didn't have a tablecloth.

"Would you like anything to drink?"

"Water, please."

Isabel handed him a metal cup with a handle. "I made some chicken soup and homemade bread," she said as placing the food in front of him. She reached for two large spoons and handed one to Charles.

His stomach suddenly made another loud crouch, and he felt embarrassed. He placed his left hand over his belly as if it helped or prevented him from more unexpected noises.

"I'm sorry ma'am. I haven't eaten today. This soup smells so delicious." He placed a spoonful in his mouth.

"On a hot day like this, hot soup is the only thing that will help you to cool down."

"How's that?"

"Just eat it while it's hot, and you'll see. You'll stop sweating." Isabel sat opposite him at her dining table in her house, looking at the strange man who entered five minutes ago. Marco had already mentioned to her that he met with a girl like no one other and that he got invited to go fishing with the girl's father. Besides, Wiley was a small town and rumors spread fast, especially about the wealthy banker who moved his family over to open his new branch here.

"Your soup is very good, Mrs. Savelli."

✦

Elizabeth placed a large blanket onto the grass under the shade, provided by a large cottonwood tree.

"Here, that's good." Annie helped her stretch out the ends of the blanket. She reached for a willow basket with sandwiches and lemonade. She looked forward to this day.

"How are my two favorite girls in the world today?" Charles sat next to his wife. "What a beautiful day!"

He let out a sigh. The opening of C.E. Newman's bank had went really well. Charles met with the employees and a bank manager, and all gave him a warm welcome. He liked to create new job opportunities for people. He made sure he checked often on how things were doing in the branches he had opened throughout Montana. While he was busy with the opening of the new bank, his wife Elizabeth and daughter Annie decided to explore the new town and surrounding areas. Charles had hired a driver for them, which made Elizabeth feel good, that despite her vision disability she could spend quality time with Annie, and through Annie's eyes she herself could see and become familiar with the small town of Wiley. Whether they enjoyed ice cream downtown or they traveled beyond town to smell the forest and have their feet tickled by the velvety grass while listening to various songs the birds provided for them, those were the times no one could take away from them. And now they were all together, in the heart of nature, spending some quality time and having fun.

Charles announced, while taking a huge bite out of his sandwich, "We are going fishing tomorrow."

Annie asked, "Where?"

"There is a wide river that runs on the edge of town, a special place, where the fish always bite."

Annie asked, "Did Marco tell you about the river?"

Charles answered, "I hope to get to know the boy better. Just want to know who my only daughter's been spending all the free time with." Charles wrapped his arm around Annie and kissed her rosy cheek.

"All right, you two, hope you won't drown yourself there!" Elizabeth joined the conversation. "These mountain waters are wide and fast; they would sweep you away in a second."

Charles could sense a bit of a worry in her voice.

⚜

Although the fresh air made Annie tired, she could not fall asleep. She laid in her bed and all she could think about was Marco. She closed her eyes, let her mind to carry her back to the afternoon, when she saw him for the first time. He was so handsome. First, she noticed the misplaced streak of curly hair that slid down his forehead and went across his eye. Then she noticed his long, sun-kissed arms. He moved the streak of hair away from his eye, then she noticed he carried a small scar above his left eyebrow. Then she studied his eyes. They were dark brown, yet Marco's eyes were gentle, almost shy. He was tall, much taller than she was. She wondered how old he could be. Was he older then her? There were so many questions on her mind. She lifted the pillow from underneath her head and placed it onto her face. She took several seconds to lift that pillow and put it back under her head. The young girl felt the blood rushing through her face. She was blushing. She caught herself smiling and when she realized that, she stopped. Annie bit her lower lip and whispered his name "*Marco Savelli.*" She reached for a piece of paper and started writing.

Chapter 9

NIGHT WHISPERER

When I look at the night skies
With my curious eyes,
My mind is mesmerized
By all the distant beauty that's letting
My humble soul open up and see
What kind of place I shall be,
A place I long to see.

I find my answer in your heart,
Just like the lit stars on the night sky,
Unsettling and bursting and constantly
Changing their glittery colors,
And I know I have found myself in you —
In your heart.

So I let my guard down,
And step on the mutual path
To see the endless lit sky with you —
My love.

The whispers at night, all angels come out to see
The happiness in me and you,
When violin plays and the universe sways
With such a grace I can't wait anymore
But come home to you, now and forever.

Chapter 10

The horse was lying down and couldn't get up. Vin knew, that's not a good sign. Usually, when a horse is down, it is going to die soon. Vin couldn't let this happen. Not yet, and definitely not this horse. This was Tuffy, his beloved companion. Although Tuffy was at the age when the inevitable was approaching, the farmer felt he had to work a miracle for him to be able to stand back on his feet. The old horse was his companion. He wasn't ready to let him go. Besides, there was too much going on that summer. The whole town talked about his daughter's Isabel's husband. People were undivided as to what really happened to Walter Wagner. Some believed he got drunk and fell into marsh at the edge of town, others said he probably drowned himself, when he was trying to get back home from the night of drinking at the local pub. And then there were those, who said that he got what he deserved, and there was only one person, who could have done it. That person was Vin Savelli. It wasn't a secret that the old Italian never grew fond of this drunk. But there used to be much happier times in the Savelli family. He remembered his daughter's smile when she met John Webb, a young, fearless man, whose heart belonged to Isabel. But this love was forbidden in Webb's family, whose powerful rich clan had inhabited Wiley for many generations. Old Mr. Wiley had different plants for his only son, and those plans didn't include a poor, farmer's girl. No one saw it coming. The tragedy happened too fast, unexpected and changed the lives of both families forever. After John's death, Isabel met and married Walter Wagner. He was a newcomer, with a possible bright future, a handsome and charming gentleman – and a big talker, whose best quality was to persuade others of his greatness. Marco was born several months later. The family lived quietly for a few years, before Wagner's demon woke up and disrupted the serene farmer's life. The older Marco grew, the more distant his father Walter became. Isabel kept telling her husband that Marco loved him. She tried her best to keep the water calm. But Vin knew better. For the sake of Isabel, he decided to swallow whatever negative feelings he had about Walter Wagner and blessed his only daughter for a marriage.

From that point on, a dark plaque spread over the Savelli's farm. When Isabel told him about Walter's drinking and violence, Vin saw only one solution that would make the black plaque go away. In his mind, he returned the sun back to the lives of those he loved and valued most in life. So for those who started spreading words about him having something to do with the disappearance of Walter Wagner, Vin quietly turned away and kept to himself. What hurt him inside was, that these words also got to his grandson and how it had affected him.

One day, Marco came up to him and told him he didn't believe any of the rumors circulating the town. "McGinnis is the worst of them all!"

"Why? Is it because he is a sheriff? He don't scare me at all!" Vin replied. "You know, Magpie, there are always three sides of the story. His, hers and the sheriffs, but it's upon you, what you decide to believe, whose side is the one that is right."

Tuffy's loud and long moan brought Vin back from his thoughts.

"I know you are hurting, my old friend," Vin said. "Please, tell me where it hurts, so that I can help you. It's not the right time to say goodbye now. Not just yet."

He stroked the horse's nose. Tuffy's breathing was elevated, but his nostrils were clean; that was a good sign, which meant the horse did not suffer from an infection. Vin lifted his lip to look at the horse's gums. He found they were in normal, pink color.

"That's good." Vin said softly. He had seen horses die and their gums were white. Not a good sign. Then he slowly checked Tuffy's stomach. He didn't find it bloated or suspended. He pressed his ear against the gut as he carefully listened for bowel movement. Even this was normal. Suddenly, the horse kicked his front leg couple of times. Vin gripped for the hoof and there he saw it. He gently pressed on the hoof, and white puss came out almost immediately.

"Now, when we know what's been bothering you, we can treat it, Tuffy." The horse answered by another load moan. Vin knew this was something that required a veterinarian. He got up made couple of steps toward the large amount of hay. He grabbed as much as he could into his arms and carried it to the horse. There, he placed the hay under Tuffy's head.

"I'll be right back," he told to the horse and rushed out of the barn. He knew only one person that can treat his old horse. Vin rushed to get help.

Doctor Timothy Jensen observed Tuffy. The veterinarian spoke slowly. "Most likely, it's an infection. From what you are telling me, it sounds like he stepped onto something while he was walking around the farm. This happens quite often. If the infection is not too deep in his hoof, I think Tuffy can recover fully. Let's get there first, and have a look." The doc opened his black leather bag, where he had all the tools; he needed to open the infected hoof. But first, he gently examined Tuffy starting at the horse's head. Just like Vin before him, Timothy raised the horse's lip.

"The gums look normal, with good pink color..." he said mostly to himself. "The eyes are nice and clear. The horse still has pretty good eyesight for his age." Then he reached into his bag to take out a stethoscope. This took a little longer than Vin would like. He scratched his scruffy face with his thick fingers nervously. Is there something going on with Tuffy's heart? Why was the doc taking so long to listen to it?

Vin couldn't hold quiet anymore. "Doc, what's going on?"

Dr. Jensen finally took out the stethoscope out from his ears.

"The damn horse has a heart strong like a church's bell," the doctor replied with a satisfying smile on his face. "Now, this is a lot of puss here in his hoof; I'll have to cut into it and squeeze as much of it as possible. He will not like it, but to cut straight into the wound is the only way to do it." Dr. Jensen looked at Vin. "We can treat the foot, while the horse is down."

Vin came behind the horse's back and knelt down behind Tuffy's head. If the horse kicked, Vin would be safe, but Jensen could take the full impact from the hoof. Dr. Jensen knew that was always a risk. Horses can be unpredictable, and when they are hurting and are in pain, anything can happen. That's just the risk he was willing to take, every time, in order to help the animals. That's why he became a farm veterinarian.

"Don't worry, Tuffy will be all right," Dr. Jensen said softly. "But you are looking a little pale there, buddy! Okay, let's see it. Oh, it's nasty, look how much puss is coming out. Ouch!"

The horse didn't even twitch. Vin watched as his friend dug into the hoof and the white, thick puss started coming out. Then the doctor reached for another tool that looked like a pliers. While the horse's foot lay on the ground, the veterinarian tried to cut out the pieces of the hoof. The whole thing started chipping and falling out together with the puss.

"That's what we want. This is good. Good boy, that's a good horse. Now, I think I got most of the nasty puss out." There was blood coming out. Tuffy started moving around. The horse did not want to hold still anymore.

"Shhh, Tuffy, it's almost done. Hold. Hold still," Vin said soothingly.

The doctor reached once again in his bag. He took out a tin can that held a special powder inside. He poured some of the powder directly on the wound.

Vin asked, "What's that?"

The doc replied, "This stops the bleeding, and...it's also antiseptic."

Vin watched as the powder mixed in with the horse's blood and the remaining puss. A few seconds later, the bleeding stopped.

"Now, I'm going to put a bandage around the foot so Tuffy doesn't get any debris in there, and you, Vin, keep an eye on the foot. Leave the bandage there for about a week. Then you can take it off. I will also shoot him with some antibiotics, and your horse should be just fine. Now we need to try to get Tuffy back on his feet."

"That'll be a challenge," Vin replied with a smile on his face. Half the battle was done. "I will get the ropes."

They tied the ropes from the horse's head to the sides of the stable, while the Tuffy was still down on the ground.

"Come on, get up. Tuffy, come on! GET UP!" Vin yelled at the horse. But Tuffy just lay there, looking at the two men standing above him.

"He's not gonna get up on his own, you know it," Dr. Jensen said jokingly. He knew how much Tuffy meant to Vin and that Vin took this very seriously. But from the doctor's point of view, he also knew that Tuffy was a stubborn horse, and if Tuffy didn't want to do something, then he just didn't do it. He had treated this horse multiple times. And so Vin stood on one side of the rope and Doc on the other. They both pulled at the same time. Finally, the horse's head lifted and after a moment, Tuffy stood on his four legs again. Or more like three and a half legs at that moment.

"He'll be all right," Doc said as he placed a handful of hay in front of Tuffy's mouth. The horse chewed the stems and snorted.

"Thanks Doc. What do I owe ya?"

"You? How about some of that beef brisket of yours..."

Vin smiled and nodded. Then both of the men left the horse alone as they exited the barn.

Marco heard all about the events that unfolded earlier that day at dinner. He felt relieved he wasn't there, because Tuffy definitely had a special place in his heart. This was a good day, after all. Tuffy was going to recover. That's all that mattered. After they were done eating, he went to the barn and gave the old horse a couple of chopped up carrots mixed in with some sliced apples. Marco quickly checked on the bandages. The horse rested his injured leg. He tapped the horse on his nose. "Good night, Tuffy. See you tomorrow." Now he became a Magpie, whose wings had to protect those, he loved the most. With that thought, he shrugged his shoulders and walked outside to get some fresh air. The secret only he knew about, was eating him alive.

"What am I going to do, Spot?" he asked his pet piglet. "Come, let's take a walk." He slightly pulled on Spot's roped leash as the two walked into the Montana's warm evening. How many times he has seen the range in the Rockies that overlooked his spread in front of him, yet every time he looked again, there was more beauty to them, something new to see and to delight on. The sun was just settling down, making a velvety haze across the wide open sky. Marco sat walked up the hill and down on a large boulder. He let go off of his emotions. Even though, there was so much beauty around, deep inside, he felt a profound sadness. He let the tears roll down his cheeks. The mountains grew blurry and salty. He felt the bitterness of the scorned heart inside of him. How much the young farmer wanted to shout it out load, how much he wanted to confine in his grandfather. If he only could to let him know what he had seen! How much he wanted to say he forgave and condoned the act of that terrible, terrible night. How much his young soul wanted to thank his grandfather for freeing his mother from the evil claws of Walter Wagner. He struggled with his inner dilemma. Should he tell his grandfather what he had witnessed or should he keep it a secret? Knowing how Vin could react, Marco chose to keep it a secret. His grandfather didn't want him to worry, and this was exactly what he was doing. He worried day and night. This would test how strong he was. On that summer evening, surrounded by nothing but nature and his pet friend, Marco made himself swear to protect his family whatever it takes. The next time Sheriff McGinnis showed up at their farm, he had to be strong. His grandfather was strong, and he had to be, too.

The second time he looked up at the sky, the sun was behind the mountains, and the air turned cold. It was time to head back to the house, before the darkness fell. He called for Spot, and the little pig came right away. The tall grass ticked Marco's bare feet, but it just felt chilly. He crossed the creek, and jumped over the rocks and into the tall grass when his eyes caught the glimpse of the feather. He bent down and picked it up. The feather was long and wide with brown and red colors. He had seen feathers like this before.

"Red Hawk," he whispered. "Must have fallen from his tail."

By the time he and Spot got back to the house, it was dark outside.

"Where have you been? You made me worried," his mother said. She dressed in a nightgown on, and her hair was braided and sat on her left shoulder.

"I'm sorry, Mom; I took Spot for a walk and didn't realize how late it got. Look what I found." He showed her the feather.

"Nice. It looks like it's from a hawk. You can sharpen the end and use it as an ink pen."

"Maybe," he said quietly. He kissed his mother good night and went upstairs. Marco placed the feather on a night stand next to him. He had a better idea for the pretty red hawk's feather.

Chapter 11

"What a beautiful morning!" Charles stretched his arms and looked outside the window.

He poured himself a cup of coffee. Black coffee, that's how he drank his cup every single morning. No sugar or milk. His lips touched the rim of the porcelain mug, and he swallowed the hot liquid. The banker got up early, looking forward to the fishing trip with Marco Savelli. Despite the rumors that spread through the small Wiley town, Charles wanted to make his own opinion about the farmer's boy his only daughter dated. Elizabeth's words echoed in his mind. *Marco is a good person,* she said. Should he give him a chance? Charles looked up at the sky, as if the answer was written up there. Time on the large kitchen clock announced five in the morning.

He gulped down another sip of the coffee and looked at the food on the table. Charles wrapped a piece of salami into a slice of white cheese. He chewed slowly, enjoying the mixed taste of the meat and cheese on his tongue. A small bird made its way on a branch overlooking the Newman's porch. The little bird made himself heard in the tones of mellow whistles.

"A bluebird..." Charles whispered.

"Where? I want to see him." Elizabeth's voice came from behind. Charles turned around, "You are up early."

"Where is the bird? Show me."

Charles took his wife's hand and walked her to the kitchen window. He leaned closer to his wife and gently whispered to her ear, "He is right there, on that branch, overlooking our porch. Look over your left shoulder."

"He is beautiful," she replied. The bluebird wasn't scared of them at all. He kept on singing his morning song, and they were his only audience. Charles placed his arms around Elizabeth as she let her head lean onto his chest.

When Marco heard the invitation to go fishing, he was ecstatic. He knew he could prove himself to Mr. Newman, and he didn't even have to work hard to do so. He has been going out fishing with his grandfather ever since he was a little boy. This is was game, and he could play it the best. He got up early and headed to the barn to check on the animals. Then he filled their buckets with fresh water, threw some straw to the feeders, and spread some grain for the chickens.

"I'm going to see the banker today. He's my girl's father." He talked to the horse. "It's going to be an awesome day." He checked on Tuffy's leg. One more day and the bandages could come off. The horse stood firmly on all four of his legs. "Good job, Tuffy." He brushed the horse's back. Marco moved over to the cow, milked it, and brought the bucket with the hot liquid back to the house where he placed it in a cold cellar.

Then he looked down and next to his feet stood the pig, watching his master's every move, curious little piglet. "I'm sorry Spot, I can't take you with me. I'll see you in the evening. You take good care of the animals, here. I'm counting on you, Spot!" Marco jumped on his bike and left the farm.

He whistled all the way to the Newman's house. Two days ago, Annie told him where their house was in town. Besides, Marco knew Wiley better than anyone else. He knew exactly who lived where. And so, when Annie told him, her father bought the old rustic place, he knew exactly, where to go. The house used to belong to Flynn and Evelyn Benton. When Mr. Benton died, Evelyn shut herself inside the house and never went out again. Since they didn't have any children, townfolks stopped by to deliver Mrs. Benton groceries and check on her from time to time. One day, when she didn't answer the door, and the locals knew this was the end of Evelyn Benton. She joined her husband in the family grave at the edge of Wiley town. Marco wasn't sure whether Annie or her parents knew these details. The Benton house went for a public sale, since there weren't any direct descendants. Eventually, Charles Newman bought it and restored the place. Marco leaned his bike on the front steps. He knocked on the door.

"Good morning, Mr. Newman."

"Good morning, Marco. You are right on time," Charles answered while placing his round watch back to his vest's pocket. Marco noticed the watch was gold and had a cover that made a light clipping sound when closed. There was a thin, golden chain that went from the vest's pocket to the watch. Marco guessed that Mr. Newman's watch must be expensive.

"Have a seat; I'll be just a minute." Charles canted his head toward the fabric chair next to the large green potted plant. "Did you have breakfast yet?"

"Yes, I ate, thank you, Mr. Newman." Marco replied as he watched Charles exit the hallway. He looked around. The house looked bigger inside than from out. The hallway had shiny white wallpaper with tones of gold and silver stripes on it. White molding framed the bottom and the top of the walls of the hall-way. There were two free-standing chairs, one which Marco sat in. The wood on the chairs was painted mahogany and the four legs were hand carved into a lion's head. The same applied for the arm rests. Marco's fingers brushed over the lion's open mouth, while he waited for Mr. Newman to come back. He wondered where Mrs. Newman was. He looked for Annie but didn't see anyone else, except his own reflection in the oversized mirror mounted on the opposite wall. The mirror's frame looked like gold. To support the heavy weight, there was a long wooden rim under that the Newman's used like a shelf. There was a single porcelain statue on it, a ballerina. Suddenly, a loud bang came from no-where. Marco jumped on the chair, then he realized it was just a sound of large clock, announcing six in the morning. God, it was early, but if one wanted to enjoy a good day of fishing, then six in the morning was the right time to be up.

"Are you ready, young man?" Charles Newman's face broke into a wide smile.

"Yes, sir!"

⚜

They parked the car at the edge of the dusty road. The time was 6:17, and the air was still and crisp. The men walked down the hill and to the river bank.

Charles looked up at the sky. "Looks like it's going to be a nice day! Not a single cloud up there." He was pleased with the forecast. Marco handed him his fishing pole. Each man carried its own willow braided bag over their shoulders.

"Oh, isn't it beautiful out here?" Charles let out a loud sigh. "It's so peaceful..." Then he turned his head over and saw Marco standing in the middle of the river. Charles realize Marco couldn't hear him anymore.

The water was wide but in no means rough. Tall pine and spruce trees surrounded both shores of the Agate River. The river bank was mixed with bigger and smaller rocks. There were even a few large boulders, some in the middle of the river, being splashed and washed over, and over again, by the cold Montana waters. The river's name was derived from the state's natural gemstone. An agate was a stone of various colors and textures. This colorful beauty was believed by the Montana people to have healing and protecting powers. The local fishermen who came down couldn't be more amazed at its powerful nature ability to look different every single day. And so, they named the river Agate. Just like the gemstone, that could carry various colors, and the river could change its appearance. If it rained, the water would wash all the way to the edges and take the little rocks with her; when the rain became sparse, the river would spit some of the rocks back to the shore, as if it was paying it back. Then when the winter came, and snow slowly fell on the rocks, trees and the river itself, the Agate changed once again. Then on one, early spring day, when the snow started melting and the sun made its way up on the sky, a little boy with his father came down to the river. The father looked away, for just a split second, when he heard the child's screams. The snow bank on the river's edge broke under the little boy's feet, and the waters swallowed his body. The father franticly ran alongside the shore, burying his feet in the partly melted snow, yelling his boy's name. All of the sudden the boy's head appeared above the water. His body stopped over one of the large boulders. His father ran as fast as he could. The water splashing over his clothes, he felt the chills and the shiver of his little son's trembling body. But the boy was alive. The father nicknamed the river Agate. The story soon spread like flies around the Wiley town. And ever since, everyone started to believe, Agate had protective powers. That summer the fish bit strong, and returned back to the cold, Montana stream.

Marco reached inside the willow bag and took out live bait. He pierced the earthworm on the fishing hook. With his right arm, he made several loops above his head before he let the nylon fish hook fall in the water. He knew what he was doing. He had done this hundred times before. But this was the first time he fished with Mr. Newman. He wanted to show him his best. Marco knew how important it was for him to make a good impression on Annie's father. He wanted to see her again. He wanted to know more about her. But if her father disapproved of him, his chances of meeting with Annie again, would be slim to none. The Agate River ran rich in trout and salmon. He looked over his shoulder. Charles Newman stood about 20 feet away from him. Marco wondered whether he has caught any fish yet. His thoughts were suddenly interrupted by a slight pull on his own fishing pole. Then another, much stronger pull came right after the first one. Marco quickly reeled the nylon back, bringing the caught fish closer to him. Then he lifted the pole into the air. There it was a beautiful rainbow trout.

He yelled, "Whoa, I got one!" He cheered and glanced at Charles Newman.

"Good job, Marco!" Charles yelled over the river's gushing waters, his left hand in the air and his thumb waived against the blue sky.

"That's one!" Marco shouted happily, as he rinsed his free hand in the water. Then he reached for the fish and released the rainbow trout from the hook. The fish jumped back into the river and was gone in a blink of an eye.

Charles Newman yelled across the water, "Why did you do that?"

Marco yelled back at him, "What?"

"Why did you release the fish back to the water? It *was* our lunch!"

"I can't hear you!" Marco shouted back. He watched Mr. Newman maneuver himself on the slippery rocks. Now, it was Charles' turn. He quickly reeled back on the fishing pole. The fish either fought hard or perhaps it was the water's stream, Charles couldn't tell, but it took him a while to fight whatever he got on the hook. Marco watched how Charles' body swung back and forth, then from left to right and then again, back and forth, as he tried to recover his catch. Marco walked over to Charles. The two men got a look at what undoubtedly was a greatest catch of the day, a single sculpin.

Marco let out a huge laugh. "It's not even an adult."

"You don't think so?" Charles held the small fish in his palm.

"Hell no! This definitely isn't over five inches long. An adult sculpin has good six full inches in length!"

"I think we should let it go, so it can grow to its full expectations."

Charles placed his palm under the clear water.

"Good try, though." Marco looked at Charles.

"Yeah...why did you let go off the rainbow trout, Marco?"

The boy thought of his answer first, before he spoke. "That's just something my grandfather has thought me. Something we sometimes do, when we go fly fishing together."

Charles sensed the opportunity to speak about Vin Savelli. "What would you say we go sit up there, on that flat boulder and eat these delicious sandwiches? I'm kind of hungry...How about you?"

"Sounds good to me."

The two sat down on the big rock's flat, smooth surface. Charles reached down into his willow bag. The inside was divided into two separate spaces, one made for the fishing bait, the other side for snacks and drinks.

"Here." He handed a wrapped slice of sandwich to Marco.

"Thank you. He took a huge bite. "Mmm, it's delicious. I'm starved."

"Listen, Marco, there is something I would like to talk to you about. It's rather...um, it's about your family."

Marco's face stiffened and his eyes grew sad. He tried to keep himself as contend and calm, as possible. "What is it you want to know?"

"I've heard people talking, spreading words about your grandfather..." Charles looked at the young farmer. The boy didn't even twitch. "I know this must be difficult for you to lose your father at such a young age...I can't even imagine, how that must feel...umm, I just wanted to let you know, if you ever need to talk, about anything, I'm here to listen."

Marco chewed the piece of sandwich in his mouth. It went from left to right and left again, before he finally swallowed it.

Since Charles didn't hear any reply to what he just said to Marco, he felt he needed to say something else, to say more. "Although, I've heard some rumors, I think they are just that. Rumors. Lies. Gossip, you know."

"I appreciate it, sir. I really do. Thank you." Marco replied calmly. "We don't know what happened. Whether he's dead or not. Sometimes he goes and is out for days. This isn't the first time he's done that."

"Hasn't it been a month?" Charles asked curiously. He took a deep breath. "I know you like my daughter, Annie."

Marco shrugged. He immediately corrected his posture and sat up higher on the boulder. The piece of bread got stuck down his throat and pain entered his chest. He coughed, but to no avail.

"Here, drink some of this." Charles unscrewed the top and handed him a flat tin bottle. The mix of sour and sweet liquid immediately picked up the stubborn stuck piece of bread and washed it down to his stomach. "Better?"

"Yes, much better. Thank you." Marco returned the tin bottle back to Charles. "Mr. Newman, I know what kinds of words are circling this small town. I've heard them myself. We all have. Please know, that my grandfather Vin is a good man. He is a hard-working farmer. He took care of his daughter – my mother – by himself and he's been taking care of me, ever since I was born. Everything I know...and everything I am today, is because of him." A gust of wind blew over and carried the last words high in the air above and down the stream of Agate River. Marco looked up and saw a thick, long, branch that came from the old and tall pine tree that grew higher above the trees that surrounded it. Perhaps because the pine's roots got all the nutrients from the river, it reached its gigantic height. There was a bird, sitting at the tip of the overhanging branch, looking at the two men. This time, Marco found himself under the magpie's wings. He felt the warm breeze around him; a feeling of comfort and peace. The corners of his lips curled up in a smile.

"I am glad Vin has a grandson like you. But, forgive me for asking you... umm, don't you miss your father? Don't you want to know, where he is, or what happened to him?"

Charles saw the sadness in the young boy's dark brown eyes. He felt for him. He didn't want to nag him with more questions. But on that day, he learned a new fact; perhaps the only fact among the rumors. Walter Wagner *was* a mystery on its own. A sudden change of mood arose from the Agate River.

"Whoa, did you see that?" Marco pointed his finger toward the river. "Was that a white fish?" We oughta get back to fishing. Let's go!"

Marco jumped from the boulder in to the rocks and down the river bank until his feet touched the cold, clear water.

"Wait up, Marco! What's the rush, to catch and release again?" Charles joked, as he followed behind Marco's steps.

They spent a few more hours at the Agate River. The untamed waters flowed in the valley between two mountain rangers, surrounded by thick forests along the sides. It was a paradise, with fresh breeze and eagles nibbling on the leftover fish that got thrown away on the edge of the river by fishermen. The brown bears would come and join the birds, but the bears always got the biggest piece, leaving the bald eagles to scavenge whatever was left behind. Even wolves came down to Agate River, especially after the long snowy winters. They fed their starved stomachs. Charles carried a gun, as he knew better. They entered the wild country, and bears could be anywhere around them. He had yet to see moose, an animal at least the twice the size of horse. Chipmunks danced on the spruce tree trunks, and foxes, weasels, wolverines and beavers lived in the area. The majestic Rockies stood in the background overlooking the forest and river life. Marco loved this peaceful place. At times, he would come here by himself and he would meditate. Vin introduced him to this serene paradise when he was just a little boy. He instantly fell in love with the tranquility and its peacefulness. *Where are the evil claws of Walter Wagner now?* Hopefully they are gone and somewhere deep, very deep in the ground.

That sunny, summer day, Charles Newman caught one brown trout, two rainbow trout. Unlike the scuplin, who got to be released back to the Agate, the trout weren't so lucky. He was happy. He needed to experience and form his own opinion about Marco.

⚜

"No fish?" Isabel asked when Marco entered the house.

"No fish," he replied carrying a smile on his face. "Catch and release."

Later that night, he wondered whether he made a good impression on Mr. Newman. Would Mr. Newman let him see Annie? Did Mr. Newman have any hesitation in regards to his grandfather? There were many questions, yet so little answers. He closed his eyes. Spot lay next to his bed on a rug. Rumors are just that. Sheriff McGinnis can't do anything without evidence. The evidence was Walter Wagner's body. There was no Wagner anymore.

Chapter 12

They played the bird game. The trick to the game was to give the competitors equal chance for winning. This required a scarf for two of the three women who were playing. Several white umbrellas served as a shade to protect their faces from the mountain sun. All the women wore long, light colored dresses. Elizabeth's dress had a straight narrow line with a lowered waist. The sleeves were long, and wide, making the dress flow and airy in the wind. From the neck down, there were four peach colored buttons, matching the color of the dress. A long, pearl necklace showed off Elizabeth's slim neck. A pair of tea drop pearls shined in her ears. The second woman had on a sleeveless dress, with a similar straight, long line like Elizabeth's. She also wore pearls, but hers were short with a tree line necklace. The third woman was Annie. She dressed in a loose skirt and a nice, blousy top. Even in the country, she liked to follow the fashion. She has seen women dressed in pants, or skirts, and she thought it was so refreshing. In fact, she wanted to wear pants today, but her mother disapproved.

"Annie, these are conservative women. Charles is a nobleman in this town. We need to represent him. I don't think wearing pants for a lovely, young girl like you, is appropriate."

"But mom, it's totally appropriate! It's 1925, and the fashion is changing — for the better! Besides, wearing a pair of trousers is so comfortable." But she wanted to make her mother happy, so she decided to put on a skirt and a light linen blouse. At least it wasn't a dress.

Mary Pope came over for the afternoon fun. She was the wife of John Pope, the bank manager at Charles Newman's bank. John and Charles became close friends and it all made sense to introduce his beloved wife Elizabeth to John's wife Mary.

"Mom, it will be fun." Annie tried to cheer up. She could understand how her mother's disability affected her social life. When Elizabeth survived the Scarlett fever and was left blind, she shut herself down, emotionally and socially. Annie was just a little girl when this happened. She went through a long recovery process, and eventually reconnected with things she used to love. This included her hobby for wild birds. Although, she could no longer see them through her eyes, she could now see them through her heart. When she recognized she could be pretty accurate to tell what bird was there just by hearing it sing, a new door opened for her. Elizabeth started feeling free of barriers. She slowly worked herself up back on her feet and soon stood firmly on the ground.

Mary and John Pope didn't have any children of their own. Instead, Mary put her motherly instincts into a puppy love. To no surprise, she showed up with Henrietta under her arms.

"I like your dog, Mrs. Pope," Annie said of the black Pekingese.

"Oh, thank you Annie, it's so nice of you. Henrietta appreciates it. Isn't that a lovely young lady, Henrietta?" She scratched behind the Pekingese's ear then placed the puppy on her own chair with a pillow on it. The Pekingese breathed heavily. Mary took a pride in Henrietta's long, velvety coat, brushing it several times a day. There was no way, she would give her a haircut, not even for the summer season. She looked at her precious puppy and moved her chair closer under the white umbrella.

"How do you keep her coat so shiny, Mrs. Pope?" Annie asked.

"Ms. Henrietta eats a raw egg every day for her lunch, mixed with rice and chicken meat," she said proudly.

"Charles, can you bring a bowl of water for the puppy here?" Elizabeth called for her husband.

"I can go get it." Annie quickly offered and rushed into the house.

"You have a lovely daughter, Mrs. Newman."

"Thank you, Mary; please call me Elizabeth."

Annie returned on the porch with a porcelain bowl filled with ice cold water. Henrietta immediately jumped down from her pillow throne and moved to the water dish.

"Are we all ready now to start the game?" Annie asked the women.

"We sure are," her mother replied.

"Yes, of course, that's why we are here," Mary said and petted her dog.

"Okay. Mrs. Pope, please place this scarf around your eyes..." Elizabeth said as she handed the pearl white silk sheet of fabric to her. "And this one is for me; I'm going also going to cover my eyes." She added as she sat down and wrapped the scarf over her hazel eyes.

"Oh, this is so exciting!" Mary Pope clapped her hands.

"And now, please let's all be quiet, so we can listen to the birds."

The tree women sat quietly on the Newman's porch, under the white umbrellas. They didn't have to wait long for their first challenge to come. The bird that landed on a nearby tree let himself known by a loud, popping sound. The sound came from the feathers, when he was landing on the branch.

"Is it a woodpecker?" Mary Pope tried her best guess.

"No, it's not a woodpecker," Elizabeth jumped in. She smiled. "It's a hummingbird."

The women took off their silky scarves. "Oh, yes, you are so right, Elizabeth." Mary replied as she looked at the tree branch. The bird sat there as if it knew, the women observed him. "Oh, he is beautiful. He is so little. Look at his sharp beak, and the colors on his feathers, hmm, truly a pretty bird."

The hummingbird had a long, dark beak. The top of his head cropped with grey and green colors, while the bird's neck proudly showed off a bright pink color that spread down in pinky streaks, like a necklace. This was called a gorget; a distinctive mark, that this hummingbird was a male. The bird was small in its size and the feathers on his wings were black. When he lifted his wings, ready to fly off to his next adventure, he showed off his white underpants.

"Henrietta, isn't that a pretty bird?" The dog didn't care for the bird's beauty and instead spread her paws on the pillow on the chair and gasped for air with her long, pink tongue that hung out of her mouth. A bubble suddenly appeared on one of her tiny nostrils. The poor dog had a hard time in the Montana summer day.

Elizabeth finally spoke. "Okay, let's try for another one."

Mary placed the white scarf back over her eyes. So did Annie. They all listened for another avian sound. The drumming sound came from a distance.

"It's a woodpecker!" Elizabeth said quickly.

"What? How could you tell so fast? I thought that someone was knocking on the door." Mary Pope didn't hide her surprised look.

"This is definitely a woodpecker," Annie confirmed. The two women took of their scarves hoping to see the bird. But the woodpecker was hidden somewhere in the crown of the trees around the house.

"Well Elizabeth, I have to tell you, you've already got this game." Mary looked at Annie first, then at Annie's mother.

"Mom, you are the winner."

"Let's play another round. I can be mistaken. Let's do one more." Elizabeth knew the chances of her to making a mistake are slim. But she was truly enjoying herself. It'd been a long time; she felt she excelled in front of others. There were several birds in the air, their sound mixed with one another. Each had something to say, a story to tell and a melody sing to. But there was only one sound that was above the other.

"Oh, this is nice! Who could this be?" Mary asked curiously.

The flutelike sound kept coming from a nearby site.

"Is that a sparrow?" Annie guessed.

"Noo, is it...could it be a sparrow?" Mary replied breathlessly, while she tilted her head toward the nice melody. Elizabeth already knew what bird came to visit them. This little creature had distinguished bright yellow feathers with a black V shaped necklace. It was no other than a western meadowlark.

"Elizabeth?" Mary turned her head toward Elizabeth, a scarf over her own eyes.

"Mother?"

"I like the melody, it's almost like the bird has a flute in his beak. Who could that be?" Mary let her inner thoughts out. Elizabeth knew, this bird was naturally shy and would most likely fly away soon. "It's western meadowlark," she finally said out load. "It's a pretty yellow bird with a black necklace on his chest."

Mary Pope and Annie took of the blindfolds. "Well, Elizabeth, you are the winner," Mary said.

"You won, mother." Annie said proudly.

✦

The men, Charles Newman and John Pope, spent the day talking about business. Charles was pleased to have a manager like John working in his bank. When he looked at his daughter, his mind suddenly slipped to Marco Savelli. He enjoyed fishing with him, but he still wasn't sure whether he should allow his daughter to hang out with him. There was just something unfinished with that family. Where was Walter Wagner? The answer lay between Marco and the old patriarch of the family, Vin Savelli. Charles promised himself to look deeper into this matter. There was nothing that bothered him more than an unanswered question.

✦

"What's in your mouth?" Marco reached down to the piglet's snout, who spat out a dead mouse. "Spot, leave it alone. That's gross."

The two were by the pond, the very same pond he brought Annie to. He couldn't get her off of his mind. He shared his thoughts about her with his grandfather. He told him about Annie's beauty and how much he enjoyed her company. Then he went on about the fishing trip he received from Charles Newman.

"Is he a good fisherman?" Vin wanted to know.

"I think he is a better banker than fisherman," Marco truthfully replied. He told Vin the story how Mr. Newman fought hard to pull the fish out, only to be a tiny sculpin. Vin laughed. He had a loud, obnoxious laughter.

Marco didn't tell him that Mr. Newman had asked him questions about his family. After all, only Marco knew, he had a secret. The secret has been eating his soul inside, but the feeling to protect his grandfather was much stronger. He knew, since he had decided to go on this journey, he had to fought it alone, deep, and only within himself inside.

"This girl, Annie, you really like her, huh?" Vin looked at his grandson.

Marco took a deep breath first, and then he let his fingers swish through his dark, long and curly hair. "Yes Grandpa, I really like Annie. She is like no one else I know. When I'm with her, I feel like anything is possible. I feel happy…I just feel good. We laugh a lot, and we talk a lot…about anything and everything…you know…"

"No, I don't. Tell me. What do you two talk about?"

And so Marco told his grandfather of how he met with Annie, of how her smile warmed up his heart and lit the sky above them. He told what he had learned about her family and what he told her about his. Then he went on how much Spot liked when she pet him and scratched him behind his ears. He told his grandfather he taught Annie about the wildflowers and how much she enjoyed it. The two generations of Savelli's, young and old, sat under the large pine tree on that warm summer day. The younger one happy, that the evil had finally left his family alone, the older one blissfully unaware that has been taken into protection under the magpie's wings.

"You are a good boy, Magpie. You make me proud." Vin tapped Marco's shoulder. Then the old farmer got up and left the pond, leaving Marco behind under the large pine tree.

✦

Sheriff McGinnis wiped out the sweat from his forehead. He put on his hat and let out a loud sigh. "How did he do it…" he mumbled under his lips, as studying his handwritten notes on the white sheet of paper. "What did he do with the body…" He reached for a blue ink pen and several times crossed the word *Isabel.* He wrote the name Marco instead. He kept staring at his notes for a minute or two. Then he cleared his throat and got up from his desk. As he walked out to his car, he carried a slight smile on his face. "Marco Savelli, of course, why didn't I think of him before? The damn Savellis, I'm gonna get you both." As driving off, he thought, *Walter Wagner what happened to you?*

✦

"I just have couple of more questions, if you don't mind Mr. Savelli..."

"Tell ya what, Sheriff?" Vin turned his back to the sheriff and started walking out, as sheriff McGinnis shouted at him the two words, that stopped Vin from walking away completely.

"Marco Savelli," Sheriff McGinnis said bluntly as he watched the old Vin's back slowly to turn around.

"What 'bout him?"

"I'd like to have a word with him. Is he here?"

"He ain't got nothing to do with it!" Vin lifted his hand and pointed his index finger at McGinnis' face.

"He has nothing to do with *what*, Mr. Savelli?" McGinnis stood firmly on the ground, his eyes staring directly into Vin's as if he tried to read what's behind them. He felt the drops of sweat coming down from underneath his hat and down on the sides his temples. He watched the old farmer turn his back at him, slowly walking toward the wooden barn.

"Go away!" Vin shouted.

"I'll be in touch!" McGinnis shouted. He reached into his vest and took out a large cotton handkerchief, wiped his forehead first, then the back of his neck. "God, it's ungodly hot this summer," he said as looking up with his squinty eyes at the blue sky. Then he walked to his car and left the road dust enter the air behind him.

"Magpie?" Vin walked into the barn and yelled for his grandson. "Magpie!" His strong voice scared Tuffy, who was tied up by his reins in the stable. "Sorry Tuffy, but sometimes it seems like I live alone on this farm." He patted the horse's back. He passed Tuffy's stable and walked outside. The bright sun blinded him for a moment. He shielded it with his palm and yelled for his grandson one more time.

A voice came from behind his back. "What's going on, Grandpa?"

Vin turned around and spread his hands wide on his hips. "There you are!"

"Is something wrong with mom?"

"Your mother is okay. McGinnis was just here. He wanted to speak to you. I told him to go away."

"Did he? Did he go away?"

"You bet.""He thinks you may know something...Maybe that you'd seen something. Magpie, is there anything you wanna tell me?"

Marco took a while to give his grandfather a one worded answer. But in that little quiet moment, he had millions of his own questions come and attack his young mind. He swept all the nagging away with one simple word. He looked firmly into Vin's eyes, "No."

"Good. Then don't you worry none." Vin tapped Marco's broad shoulders. "Time to get to work now, because—"

Marco quickly jumped in to finish his grandfather's sentence, "Because the animals won't wait." The two men walked side by side, one resembling the other in the fast confident pace as they headed to feed the stock.

I'll keep you safe, right here, under the magpie's wings.

⚜

On that same hot sunny afternoon, Annie took her mom to one of her favorite places in town. She held her hand as she led her up the hill through the tall grass and many colorful wildflowers.

"Oh, dear, let me catch a breath." Elizabeth stopped as she placed her hand over her chest. A big fly found its way to the Newman's girls and decided to make a hell for what it seemed to be lovely afternoon. Elizabeth vigorously waved both of her hands in front of her face in hopes of shooing the fly away. She wore all white dress with a wide skirt that covered her thin ankles. To protect her pale skin from the Montana sun, Elizabeth put on an oversized white hat. Now, the fly made its way under the hat and drove the woman crazy.

"Go away, go *away*." She franticly spanned her body in the air. "Oh Annie, why is it that I always get attacked by all sorts of bugs and you don't get any on you. Not a single one!"

"I don't know, Mother. Father says you must have a sweet blood." Annie laughed as she watched her mother's fight with the big fly.

"Where is it? I can still hear it buzz around my ears. It's so annoying."

"Here," Annie clapped her hands in the air. "It's gone — forever."

"Oh no, did you kill it?"

"Sure I did. It's a fly, mother."

"It *was* a fly."

Annie wiped her hands in the grass and wished that there was a creek she could wash away the remaining stain that the insect left behind."Come on, Mother, we are almost at the top of the hill," she said as she hooked her right pinky into Elizabeth's. When they got to the top, Annie found a nice, flat area for them to sit down.

"Ahh, there is so much beauty around here." Elizabeth gasped as she turned her head around. "Tell me Annie, what do you see?"

Through her daughter's eyes, Elizabeth saw the valley's beauty that surrounded them. "There is a large lake to the left of us. It's called Adoette Lake. It's named after the Indian girl that was born there under a single large tree. Adoette means *large tree* in native language. Then there are endless meadows full of flowers in full bloom behind the lake. I think the Savellis own that piece of land there."

"You mean Marco Savelli's family?"

"Yes, Mother. Then there are the railroad tracks on the very right."

"Oh, the loud whistling train that never fails to wake us up at three in the morning." Elizabeth didn't hide her dismay. She couldn't understand why the conductor had to blow the whistle every time he passed Wiley. The town itself was so small, with only one railroad crossing that was far away from everything.

"What else is there, Annie? Go on."

"I can see dad's bank from here. And the town's grocery store. And there is *an elephant*." Annie said almost in whisper.

"An elephant?" Her mother repeated in disbelief.

"Yes, it looks like a circus arrived in town. I see horse carriages and small people walking around." Annie stood up in hopes to get a better view. "Midgets."

"Sounds like fun," Elizabeth replied. And so on that hot, sunny afternoon Elizabeth Newman saw the town of Wiley Montana through her daughter's eyes. From the Adoette Lake to the beautiful, widespread meadows, majestic high peaks of the Rockies all the way to the midgets that came in with their circus to create smiles on children's faces.

"It's your turn; close your eyes now," Elizabeth said.

Annie shut her eyes and let her head fall down in the grass. They both became quiet, but not for long. Soon enough they were greeted with the presence of a cheerful song with a high note that started with a simple whistle and quickly changed into a colorful song. Elizabeth was blind but not deaf. She described the songbird to her daughter.

"He is small; you can hide him in your palm. He's got a black cap and bib. He has adorable white cheeks and grayish colored wings. The rest of his feathers are mostly in yellow color."

"A meadowlark?" Annie guessed.

"Nope. Try again."

"Hmm, is it a sparrow?"

"Oh come on Annie, don't underestimate this little precious beauty for a sparrow."

Annie in her all honesty couldn't tell what type of songbird it is. Maybe, if she could get a look at the bird, she would be able to name it correctly.

"Is it a chickadee?"

"Yes! Did you look?"

"No...Yes, Mother, I looked."

The women sat in the grass, up on the hill overlooking the small mountain town. They let the beautiful surroundings be their company.

Chapter 13

"What's the matter? You look like you've just seen a ghost." Annie joked and smiled at the same time. When she didn't hear any answer, her smile disappeared and her face frowned. "Marco?" She placed her right hand over his back and onto his shoulder. Marco's heart was beating fast. Annie leaned forward and looked deeply into his dark brown eyes. "What is it?" Her face grew tight with concern.

Marco cleared his throat. "I...I thought, I saw someone I know...someone I *knew*." There they were, surrounded by the happy faces around them on that Sunday afternoon. They all came to this place to get ice cream in a cone and pop sodas, and the children eager to get their hands on the giant elephant and other zoo animals, others came to see the freaks, and the sword swallower, the magician and the trapeze lady, while others were just curious, because they've never seen a real midget with their own eyes. Today was the day to see it all, here in the odd world of circus. Marco looked around him, trying to catch the glimpse of the man, who caused him this rapid heartbeat. His eyes quickly shifted from left to right and back again. Did he really see a ghost? Or perhaps were his eyes playing trick on him? Could he blame himself for being exhausted? After all, summer is a busy time, especially on the farm. The voices around blended together, he tried to put a smile on his face for Annie's sake, but his cheeks felt frozen.

"Oh my God, oh my God?! Look at the elephant, wow! Look how tall he is!" a woman sitting behind them exclaimed as the majestic animal entered the small, round arena below them. The elephant walked slowly, tilting his head on sides, greeting its audience. Then he stopped and lifted his front large paws, waving his ears in the air. His master walked in front of him holding a rein in his hand that was attached to the elephant's head. Everyone in the crowd seemed mesmerized by the giant beauty. The show was about to begin.

"Ladies and gentlemen, welcome to the Cirque de Luna. What you are about to see is extremely dangerous. You may even want to cover your eyes." The man dressed in long white overall, with a hand-sewn colorful beads and a thick, red fabric belt announced to the anxious audience. A white turban sat on his head and his eyes were marked with black eyeliner. His bearded face hid his lips. "Ladies and gentlemen, the one and only elephant, Rosie!" the turban man introduced the next performer and left the center of the round stage. The crowd quieted, and all eyes were on the three performers. Rosie, the noble elephant, lowered her back and a slim woman jumped up in the saddle. The elephant lifted herself up walked around the arena. Rosie had a beautiful red and golden blanket on her back. A necklace of golden chains and coins covered the animal's head. The thin lady on the top of Rosie's back was dressed in red, black and white dress. A male performer joined them and filled the air with exotic music. His head was wrapped in a black turban, his face was painted black and the man had a long, dark beard touching his chest. He wore a white, long, wide-sleeved shirt and a black thick belt made out of fabric. His black pants were equally wide as his shirt. Rosie, the elephant moved to the rhythm of the flute. The music was addictive, leaving an imprint on the spectators' minds. Annie found herself moving to the inviting sound of the flute, rocking her shoulders from side to side. The crowd watched as the thin woman on Rosie's back tapped the elephant on the back and it stopped. Then the turban man extended his arm toward Rosie, who picked up the flute in her mouth. A sound of music entered the stage again. Some people in the audience started laughing; some shook their heads in disbelief. Rosie the elephant was now playing the flute. The little children giggled, some clapped, some watched with their mouth opened. Some adults nodded, while others just made remarks of disbelief. They all sure attended a circus. The thin lady whispered something into Rosie's ear. The sound of the flute suddenly ended. The man with his black-colored turban lay down on the ground. He placed his head on the pillow. The air in the rounded tent got thicker as the crowd nervously watched the next performance. Rosie made several steps closer to the turban man. Then she raised her front left paw in the air. The audience gasped, some women placed their hands over *their* chest, while others covered their eyes. The elephant's foot didn't stay long in the air. After several seconds, Rosie lowered her huge foot and placed it nowhere else but on the top of the head of the turban man. For what seemed like an eternity, no one has said a word. Rosie's paw remained on the man's head, and then the flute sound cut the thick air like a sharp razor. Some people shrugged in discomfort. Who was playing the flute now? Was the man still alive? *Nothing is as it seems.* The words of the turban man echoed in Marco's ears.

"I can't watch this anymore." Annie gasped, holding her hand over her mouth, then, moving it up and covering her eyes, just to leave a narrow space between her index and middle finger. The thin lady sitting on Rosie's back stood up and made a swan pose. The audience leaned forward. The top part of the picture so beautiful and relaxing with soft tones of the flute in the air, and the thin ballerina, fragile yet so pure on the top of the back of the largest animal many people have ever seen, the bottom of the picture so wrong with the elephant's foot on the head of turban man. *Ladies and gentleman, this could be your life. It's your choice. You can either be happy and carefree, like the ballerina on the top, or you can be crushed by tons of weight in the matter of seconds, like the turban man down below. You choose.*

Marco's eyes looked behind Rosie the Elephant, farther and deeper in the audience across the stage. His eyes landed on the man in the second row. He could swear this was the man he saw before. He wasn't a ghost. He was flesh and blood right there, in front of him, watching the same freak show. A sharp pain like a blade made its way inside of his stomach. Marco tried to concentrate on the man across the stage. While others breathlessly watched the elephant show, his eyes were mapping the mysterious man sitting in second row. Due to the dimmed light inside the circus tent, Marco couldn't tell whether the man's hair was black or brown, but he could see the hair was straight with the heavy banks falling down way under the man's eyebrows. He had a beard, but he looked very familiar. The man made several moves with his hand to move the bangs out of his eyes, a gesture, well known to Marco. Every time there was about to be an outburst of anger, he would nervously comb his banks with his palm, and it would always slide right back across his eyes. A sudden chill washed over Marco's body. Walter Wagner is dead. So, were his eyes just playing a trick on him now? Which one was it? The simple truth was that no-one has found Wagner's body, so there was a possibility of him being alive. "That can't be true," Marco whispered.

"What can't be true?" Annie whispered back.

"This. All of this."

The audience's loud applause filled the circus tent. Many happy faces clapped, and some even whistled and yelled, "Bravo!" to Rosie the elephant, its ballerina, and the turban man.

"She was awesome!" Annie cheered as the crowed lifted from their seats and headed for the exit. Marco hoped to see the man closer at the exit gate, but there were just too many people around. Strike two for the mystery man, he thought.

"Who's that woman?" Annie canted her head toward the old, expensively dressed lady with an overlarge hat on her head. "She's been looking our directions for a while. I think she is looking at you!"

Marco recognized her. He waved at the old woman, but she quickly shied away and blended with the crowd. "That's Mrs. Webb. My mother knows her. She used to visit her at her house. Mrs. Webb likes our sheep cheese, but I don't really know her."

Annie's face lit with happiness. "Thank you for such a nice day." Two cute dimples showed up on her pinky cheeks.

Marco knew he was in love. He undeniably was falling for Annie, and he didn't want anything to stop him from this beautiful moment. He leaned forward and kissed her. "I can't wait to see you again."

She laughed. "But you will see me tomorrow."

"Tomorrow is a long time for me."

He walked Annie back to her house then decided to take a stroll before he would return back home to the farm. As he passed the tall meadow grass and watched the sun fall down behind the Rocky Mountains, he replayed the events of the stormy night again in his head. He knew what he had witnessed. Walter Wagner lay dead on the kitchen floor in the house. He saw the bloody shovel. What he didn't see was his grandfather Vin. On that morning, after the stormy night ended, he couldn't find his grandfather anywhere. There was no way the mystery man he saw today was his father, simply because Walter Wagner didn't exist anymore. Or did he?

✦

Chapter 14

Elizabeth, despite her vision disability, loved to cook. Even though she had staff to prepare food, she liked to do some cooking on her own. Today, she wanted to surprise Charles. She knew Annie will be starved once she gets back from riding her horse Digby. She felt really good that day. At first, moving to Wiley was rather scary for her. She's always had a hard time getting use to new places. That was even before she became blind from the Scarlett fever. But now, after few months in this small and so beautiful mountain town, she found her confidence. She knew her only daughter is in love, and that her husband Charles had done something useful for local people, giving them jobs. Life seemed to be good.

Elizabeth opened the two-sided double door white Frigidaire refrigerator. Her long, thin fingers touched the top shelf first. She felt the cold glass bottle filled with milk in her hands. She took it out and placed it on a table next to the refrigerator. She reached back into the fridge and tapped her hand on the top self until she her fingers felt the oval, smooth shell of an egg. She took two eggs and placed them on a plate next to the milk glass. "Now, where is the fish?" she muttered under her lips. When she couldn't find it on the top shelf in the refrigerator, she kneeled down and let her hand search through the bottom shelf. That's when her maid Lucretia entered the kitchen.

"Misses Newman!" Lucretia rushed to her.

"I'm all right. No worries. Just trying to find the catfish Charles caught earlier this morning. Can you help me find it?" She got up and brushed off her skirt with her hands.

"Of course, Mrs. Newman." Lucretia looked inside the double-sided refrigerator and instantly handed a plate that carried the freshwater fish. "There it is. I'm going to put the plate next to your milk and eggs, right here on the kitchen counter, Mrs. Newman." Lucretia placed the porcelain plate hit the kitchen counter.

"Thank you, Lucretia. I can now manage myself," Elizabeth replied. She didn't need anyone to feel pity for her.

Lucretia exited the kitchen as Elizabeth moved to the pantry and took out a jar of cornmeal, garlic and three large potatoes. The catfish recipe was fast and simple. She learned it from her mother when they lived in Louisiana. Her husband and daughter loved the Southern comfort food. She felt the rough lemon skin under her hands. She rolled the lemon on the kitchen counter back and forth several times, until it got softer, then she sliced it and the fresh citrus smell mixed with the air in the kitchen. She squeezed the juice using the other hand as a sieve, to avoid any seeds coming down the bowl. After she washed her hands, she added cold milk, followed by two raw eggs in the bowl. She whipped the liquid with a fork for a few seconds, to make sure the eggs got beaten well into the milk and lemon liquid mixture. Elizabeth let her hand in the air over the counter, until her fingers came across the soft needle of fresh rosemary. She kept it in a glass filled with water. That way the rosemary lasted for days. She shook it in the air, and then she broke it into several pieces in her hands and let it go down into the mixture. She crushed the glove of garlic, and added it in the bowl once again mixing everything together. Now the mixture was ready for the catfish. Charles had already cleaned the fish, so she just placed it in the bowl, and tapped the fish fillet with the tips of her fingers, to make sure, they are well soaked in. She covered the bowl with a piece of cloth and moved it back in the refrigerator. She rinsed her hands with cold water and moved onto the potatoes. Her fingers worked fast, peeling the skin of the tree large pieces. She placed the potatoes in a large pot and filled it with water. Elizabeth moved quickly in the kitchen, as she salted the pot and turned it on. One would never guess the woman was completely blind. Few minutes later she heard the stove bubble, as the diced potatoes boiled. She took out a large skillet, a butter stick and finally the soaked fillet from the fridge. That's when Lucretia returned back to the kitchen.

"Let me know if you need any help, Mrs. Newman," Lucretia said as watching Elizabeth pour the cornmeal into a deep plate.

"I'm not crippled, Lucretia, I'm just blind." Elizabeth face lighted with smile. "But you could tell me if the fillets are ready to be grilled..."

Lucretia's dark hand disappeared under the light milk and lemony liquid. She took out one fillet, shook it in the air and placed it on a plate. "It's ready," she said with her deep, Southern accent. She's been faithful to Mrs. Newman now for over fifteen years. She knew the Elizabeth who could see, she knew the process of her becoming gravely ill by taking care of her during the hardest times of Scarlett fever, she knew her slowly recover and overcoming the greatest obstacles, as living through the first months of her blindness. The two women bonded even more during the hard times, making their relationship one of a kind. The rich madams of the high society many times pointed out this unusual friendship to Elizabeth, telling her it wasn't not right to treat her black servant with so much respect and kindness.

Elizabeth placed a generous amount of butter on a large skillet as Lucretia watched the cube slowly melt under the hot stove. Meantime she took one piece of the catfish and dipped it in the cornmeal flipping it the other side and coating it evenly with the salted mixture. Then Lucretia looked over and told Elizabeth the butter was fully melted and the skillet ready for the fish to fry. As soon as the breaded piece of catfish hit the hot buttery skillet, a sizzling sound entered the kitchen.

The smell of garlic and rosemary with a hit of lemon made Elizabeth's mouth water. "Yummy," she said as she tried to find a fork.

Lucretia came quickly to her help and Elizabeth tried if the boiling potatoes are soft enough. "Not just yet." Lucretia started humming a song well known to Elizabeth. She used to sing it every day to Annie, when she was a child. Where did all that time go? *God loves us all, whether you are big or small, the Sun warms your soul, go catch the branch that hangs low, with love that touches your heart, so be smart and take it with a pride, God loves us all, forever and some more.* She joined Lucretia, and the two women carried on the tune throughout the summer kitchen, while frying garlic and rosemary lemon catfish with mashed potatoes. Elizabeth felt alive, the inviting smell spread out of the window, just in time Annie returned from a ride with her beloved horse Digby. She heard her mother's loud laugh, so contagious, that it warmed up her heart and Annie's own lips curled up in a wide smile. She loved when her mother cooked. As Annie's steps came closer to the kitchen, the dynamic between the women suddenly changed.

Lucretia's deep, Southern voice said, "I've heard the rumors, Mrs. Newman, about the Italian farmer and his grandson. The whole town talks about the family."

Annie stopped and stood there looking into the kitchen from the open doorway. She saw the back shoulder of her mother, leaning over the stove, as Lucretia's poured the boiling water from potatoes down the kitchen's sink. The steam came up over Lucretia's face, who wiped the forehead with her dark arm.

"Someone saw Walter Wagner in town," Lucretia continued. "They said he's changed a lot. They said his face is now covered with a long, and ungroomed beard that covering a deep, long scar on his face. A scar that meant to kill him."

Annie's heart sank and her face became pale. She placed her right palm over her chest. She took several deep breaths. On the other side of the doorway, Elizabeth's posture seemed calm, still leaning over the hot stove, turning the catfish from one side to another. Annie wanted to scream, but her throat was dry. *Can't you hear what Lucretia just said? Say something. Anything. Please!* Annie's thoughts buzzed in her head like a swarm of wild bees. Elizabeth finally turned around. "I don't believe in rumors. Who was the man that says he saw Wagner?"

Annie didn't hear Lucretia's reply. She quickly exited the house out into the Montana fields. She ran as fast as she could, until she felt a sharp pain in her right hip. She stopped at the edge of the Agate River, where her father and Marco fished about a month ago. Her face saddened and tears came down her rosy cheeks. *Caw-caw!* A raven flew above the river and chased the eagle away. She watched as the blackbird tirelessly followed behind the eagle's tail, getting higher and above the larger bird and with his sharp beak attacked the eagle in flight. She's never run so far away from her home. The cold air from the water made her shiver. She decided to go back to her house. She thought about the old woman that kept looking at Marco when they exited the circus tent. She wished she knew more about her.

⚜

Trudy Webb became a widow just over a year before. She became a sole beneficiary in her husband's estate, inheriting all 400 acres of land and sheep farm business. The lamb pastures covered the Montana's land for generations. Old Mr. Webb took over his father's business, and always hoped to one day to give it to his own son. They sell the meat, using nearly everything from the sheep's body. They cut open the dead animals and took out their stomachs; they would then place them on scale and weight each piece, documenting everything in writing. They would sell the wool beyond the Montana borders, to those who transformed it into clothing, the skin into shoes, and handbags. All that remained were the sheep's bones. It was a lucrative market, a business that made a lot of money. But only Vin Savelli, had that kind of sheep, that produced milk from which The Savelli farm made a breaded sheep cheese. Many times the old Mr. Webb visited the Italian's farm, offering him a plenty of dollars for a sheep of his own. But the stubborn farmer never accepted any of the money offers. The all well realized, the sheep on his farm meant more to him, then just a piece of meat, skin, or stomach or ribs. When Mr. Webb died, his wife Trudy sold all the sheep to those, who promised to treat the animal with respect. She gave some to Vin Savelli for free. The rest was divided between other locals or traveled far through the vast land of Montana, perhaps even beyond its border.

Life had its own plan and blessed them with one healthy son. Trudy Webb was a tough cookie with a sharp mind. Although she was a petite woman, she carried her head high and never let her emotions known out loud. She liked to wear pants long before this fashion came into popularity amongst women, and her tongue sometimes cut a slack with most of the men. She earned respect quickly, and men in Wiley preferred to keep far away from her, unless it concerned the sheep business. But even then Trudy usually got what she wanted. She always combed her now gray hair into a loose bun, leaving few slightly curly strands on the sides of her temples. Her blue eyes still sparkled and looked like they were reading right through you. She was never seen in public without wearing a makeup. A red lipstick lined her lips, with a touch of rose on her cheeks. Black mascara brought up her long eyelashes and let noticed her blue eyes. Her late husband once said, that if frost could cover the blue sky, that's because Trudy's eyes made it. The noble woman reached for a china cup and took a sip of hot tea. The corners of her lips curled in a smile. She was glad to see Marco again. Of course she knew about rumors. Trudy was ready to step in and change everything. This time, everyone around better be ready.

Chapter 15

The arrival of September brought all sorts of beautiful colors to Montana fields. The rich and luscious green mountains slowly transformed into the parade of red, orange and yellow shades. The first birch trees turned the green leaves into a golden blanket that grew bigger with each day as autumn had already arrived and the night temperatures decreased. However, some of the wildflowers were still in full bloom, like Indian paintbrush, with its tall, fiery red color, that stood out in the vast fields. Wild berries like crowberries, blueberries and cranberries made for local harvest a busy month. Marco's mother Isabel waited for the first morning frost, which would make these berries bring out the sugar and make them sweeter. The cool overnight temperature would make the berries soften up, and the acid inside would turn to sugar. Unlike the seasonal berries, the crowberries stayed on ground bushes throughout the winter, under the snow. They served a broad purpose for the wildlife, when other food was vast, the animals could dig through the snow, and feed on these round, black and juicy berries. Marco walked up the steep hill, until he reached a saddle. He sat down on the large, but flat boulder. The afternoon sun warmed the otherwise cold stone, making it now nice and comfortable. He looked at the Hidden Lake in front of him. The first day his grandfather showed him this trail was when he was five or six years old. At that time, the lake didn't have any name.

"But doesn't it feel lonely, Grandpa?"

"What do you mean, Magpie?"

"Can we give it a name?"

This memory seemed so fresh, as if this happened just yesterday. He no longer was that little boy. He became a tortured soul now. And one, that was *tragic and irreversible*. He felt angry, he felt vulnerable. Marco covered his face with his hands, and then let his fingers brush through his raven colored curly hair. Tears rolled down his cheeks. He finally let go and cried until his eyes became a pond of salty sorrow. His companions were nature, plants, and birds. The breeze grew stronger and became wind and the wind brought clouds that covered the blue sky. The air smelled like rain. The sky joined in, and wept with the young boy's soul. But with the rain, certain liberation came along. Marco spread his arms, with his palms toward the endless sky, tilted his head back and yelled out loud from his lungs. He let the beating rain wash away everything from his past, until nothing remained and the demon dissolved and no longer existed in his mind. Soon after, the sky broke the dark clouds, and the first sun beams shined onto the Montana valley like a liquid gold. Marco looked up and there he saw a beautiful double rainbow. The three colorful lines of red, yellow and green from the top of the sky all the way down behind the Rocky Mountains, making it into a spectacular view on the Hidden Lake that September afternoon. Marco took off the soaked shirt. He raised both of his arms up toward the sky. He hugged the double rainbow and let out a loud laugh. He felt as if the past didn't matter anymore, and now, there was only the future that he had to look up to. He would never ever fear Walter Wagner in his life, ever again. He, his mother and his grandfather were all it mattered now. Liberated, freed, however you wanted to call it.

A loud cracking sound interrupted the overwhelming quiet place. A herd of the Canadian geese made its way through the rain, sun and the double rainbow and decided to land on the Hidden Lake. Marco's heart delighted with the presence of the company he just earned. He sat up higher on the boulder and watched as the geese descended one after another down on the lake. The large birds put on their brakes, spread the wings wide, and glided down through the air, then the bird's feet touched the water, and skid across until their wings folded and it floated on the mountain lake. One goose after another made this descend, until the herd was united again. Then the birds started their washing ritual. A sound of flipping feathers splashing on the water echoed in the air. Marco watched in amusement, as the birds head and neck dove under the clear mountain water. What a joy to watch these geese to take a bath. They rolled from one side to another, then they splashed the water with their wide wings again, head under water, and head above the water, blissfully unaware of their human presence. Where did they come from? Perhaps they just flew in from Canada. They made a stop here, to rest and refuel with fresh green grass, before heading south for winter. Marco felt fascinated by these wild birds. A certain unknown magic surrounding the geese made him to watch them every fall. A bird parade he looked forward to year after year, ever since he was a little boy. Sometimes he wished he could join them and follow them wherever they went. He wanted to be free like them. This time, this year, this very moment he wanted to stay. He no longer desired to join the birds on their journey. Now, he only had people here he adored, like his mother Isabel, his grandfather and Annie. "Travel safe!" He waved at the geese. Marco carried his shirt in hand and walking down through the tall mountain grass, pass the Indian paintbrush and other wildflowers toward his home.

✤

Officer Hanson put a dirty, soiled bag on the hard wood floor in McGinnis' office. "Here it is!" he said darkly, and then he firmly pressed his lips together. Sheriff looked at the fabric bag, and then he asked the officer to leave him alone. After the door shut, McGinnis leaned down and carefully opened the bag. A telephone call woke him up early that morning, informing him, that a local person found a suspicious item lying in the plains, close to the swamps. The man who found the soiled bag was hunting for ducks, when he stumbled upon it. He brought it back to town with him, and made the call to the local police station. McGinnis often stayed at his office overnight, falling asleep on his desk. The ringing phone woke him up at 5.30 in the morning. He immediately thought of Walter Wagner. Now, looking at the dirty bag, he hesitated for a second. Could there be a body part? McGinnis' stomach turned sour with that thought. He hasn't had breakfast yet. The bag was about 4 feet tall, and 3 feet wide. The bag wasn't heavy, so McGinnis immediately eliminated the option of a corpse. A single string tied the top of the fabric. There were no other markings or labels on it. He didn't recognize seeing a bag in any Wiley store. His body leaned over and closer as he carefully pulled on the dirty string. The sheriff's eyes widened to see what's inside, when at the same moment a loud knock on the door made him startle. "Jesus Christ, seems I can't be left alone for a minute!" He wiped the nervous sweat from his forehead.

Officer John Hanson stood in the doorway. "I got some hot coffee and doughnuts. My wife made them last night!" He raised the paper bag in the air and smiled at his boss. When no reply came, he asked, "Have you had breakfast yet?"

McGinnis reached for the paper bag, and smelling the doughnuts, his mouth watered with saliva. He'd never married or had a girlfriend. The sheriff preferred to live alone, and locals even called him *loner*. He didn't care. He liked the freedom of not taking care of anyone else, the freedom of not having a responsibility for anyone but himself. But there was something about John's wife, Grace. He had a soft spot for her in his heart and kept it a secret. He sat down behind his desk and took a deep bite of the doughnut. The soft raspberry jelly coated his tongue like velvet. Tart at first, the homemade jelly turned sweet with the doughy mixture.

"Good, you like it?" John Hanson asked, still standing in McGinnis' office.

"Mmm, it's delicious! Best breakfast for this crazy morning. Tell Grace..." *I love her,* his mind whispered. "...tell your wife thank you from me."

The officer straightened up and smiled back at McGinnis. "Will do, sheriff. Grace will be happy to hear that."

McGinnis' leg kicked the bag he hid under his desk. An unpleasant feeling went through his body like a lightning bolt. He swallowed the last piece, licked the raspberry jelly off of his index finger and took a sip of the hot, black coffee. He took a deep breath and pulled on the string from the top. He looked inside. Sheriff felt his heart pumping faster and his breath getting deeper, as he leaned forward toward the dirty bag. There was no odor. No blood. He stuck his hand inside. "Bone," he said breathlessly. McGinnis looked closer at the piece of the jaw that had a portion of teeth still attached to it. He flipped the back upside down and let it spill on the floor. Something moved and made the sheriff jump. He dropped the empty bag on the floor. "What the hell was that?" He looked down and saw a frog making its way across the office floor. His eyes crossed the items that fell out of the bag. "What am I supposed to make out of this? Someone took of his hat, shoes, and a shirt and placed it in a fabric bag, together with a jaw bone from some animal and then tossed it all out in the fields behind Wiley?" McGinnis spoke out loud, but he was the only one in the room. He got no answers. Walter Wagner was still missing, and Vin Savelli still walked free. Did the clothes belong to Walter Wagner? McGinnis sat down behind his desk and dialed a number on his phone.

A pleasant, soft woman's voice answered. "C.E. Newman Bank, this is Mary, how can I help you?"

"This is Sheriff McGinnis, I need to speak to Charles Newman. Is he there?"

"I am sorry, Mr. McGinnis, but Mr. Newman is out of town."

"What?"

"He will be back on Thursday. Would you wish to leave a message for him?"

McGinnis nervously tapped on the desk with his left hand. Thursday was three days from today.

"Sir?"

"No, no message." McGinnis said quickly and hung up the phone. Then he returned all the items back into the bag, tied the knot on the top, and walked outside the police station. He drove to Savelli's farm. When he arrived, he saw Marco walking out of the barn, carrying a bucket in his hand. He walked toward the young boy.

Marco stopped and set the bucket full of freshly milked cow's milk next to him on the dirt path. He tried to remain calm. "How can I help you, Sheriff?"

"Is your mother home? Or you grandfather? I just want to ask some questions. I won't be long."

"No, I'm afraid they are not here. Is there something you would like to ask me?"

"Hmm, they are not here. So, it's just you, this morning?" The sheriff didn't hide the irony in his voice.

"What do you want?" Marco asked. Horses feet stamped in the background. "I'm busy."

"There is something I want to show you." McGinnis opened the bag and took out the shirt and then the hat. He lifted his arms in front of the young boy. "Do you recognize these?"

"No." Marco said sharply.

"*No,*" the Sheriff repeated. "Okay, well, what about these shoes, do they look familiar to you?"

"No, they don't." Marco's face turned away, and he swung his arm and lifted the bucket and walked to the house. He stopped short in front of the entrance and shouted loudly, "Go away!"

"I'll be back." McGinnis said before he jumped back into his car. He wiped the sweat from his face into his shirt. "Damn hot day!"

✦

Marco carried on with his day, regardless of the sheriff's visit that morning. After he milked the cow, he let the rest of the animals out of the barn, and into the fenced area, where they remained for the rest of the day. He shoveled and removed the old straw, replacing it with a fresh one, and then poured water into several buckets and placed straw into the feeders. He collected fresh eggs; they were all brown in color and some of them still warm from the hens feathered bodies. He returned to the house, where he placed several thin slices of wood into the stove with an old paper then lit the match. He closed the iron door and reached into the cabinet for the chicory coffee. The young farmer placed two spoons into a mug. The aroma of the brown, coarse ground mix entered his nose. Marco put a kettle of water on the woodstove and waited for it to come to boil. In the meantime, he sliced two thick cuts of bacon and cut a generous amount of bread on the plate. He took the iron pan and fried two eggs with salt and pepper. The whistling sound of the kettle let him know the water was brewing. He poured the hot, steamy water over the chicory mix then watched the mix rise to the top of the cup. He took a spoon and stirred the dark liquid. Soon, the mix fell down to the bottom of the cup. He added fresh cow milk.

His mother and his grandfather had taken off early, traveling to another town to attend the wool sale. They did this every year. The profit from the sheep's wool would carry them through the most of the winter, providing a living for them and their farm animals. He then enjoyed the scrambled eggs with bacon and bread. From around the corner and across the hallway the snorting sound came. The pig limped his way to Marco's chair and lifted his nose.

"Spot. Here you are, you sleepy head." Marco scratched the pig behind his ear. Then he placed a hardboiled egg on the floor. Spot chew it fast and wanted more. "You lucky pig!" He said warmly. The young farmer thought of this morning's visit. He was sure, he made a good job not to let sheriff know, he recognized the pieces of clothing. The emotions flooded his mind and all the images from that stormy night invaded his brain. It's been over two months of Wagner's disappearance and the town folks still talked about him. But no one really missed him. Isabel explained that he probably left town in search of a better place, as he no longer liked the farm. Vin didn't talk about him at all. Whenever he was approached by someone, the corners of his lips curled up into a slight smile, politely giving an answer to whoever had a question. Many times Marco wanted to share his secret with his mother, thinking that perhaps the heavy burden would lighten a bit if he just simply shared it with someone he trusted. Other times he contemplated if it was right and ethical to approach his grandfather about what he had witnessed. What would Vin tell him? Knowing his grandfather all his life, he knew this wasn't an option for him. Vin would tell him to go to the authorities, and by authorities he would mean police. And that would mean letting McGinnis win. And Marco could in no circumstances allow this to happen. One thing he learned from his beloved grandfather was to remain faithful to his family, to his only roots. He would fight to keep his family together, and the best kept secret was the one that remained hidden from the rest of the world. He would just have to find a way to cope with this fact and accept the situations that may arise in the future. His grandfather's life was worth more. If not for his grandfather, Wagner would be alive now, but his mother would be dead.

Like a dark cloud on the windless sky, one unanswered question still remained. What happened to Wagner's body? Did Vin burn it? That's what Marco would do. But then there wasn't any fire or smoke, as he remembered. Did his grandfather dig a hole somewhere in the woods and just dumped the monster in it? Or did he drive the lifeless drunk on his horse carriage out of town and throw him someplace in the Montana prairie for wolves to feed on? And finally, was McGinnis that smart to put the pieces of the puzzle together to figure it out?

What's the right thing to do? Should he make a confession? Who should he confine to? There are really only two people in the entire world that he could trust: his mother and his grandfather. Is the best secret the one which is kept hidden?

"Oh, Spot!" He looked back at the piglet. So much had changed; the home became quieter and peaceful. Isabel found her smile again; how refreshing and joyful for all of them. The sun came through the windows and warmed the kitchen. There was no rush anymore. Vin did everyone a favor, and as far as Marco was concerned he would do the same. *To hell with you, Wagner!* Marco stood up and brushed off breadcrumbs off of his pants. "Let's go for a walk." The piglet followed him out the door into the dusty yard and stopped short and snorted. "Come on, Spot." Marco turned and called for the pig. "All right. Stay then."

The young farmer ran across the mountain meadow when he stumbled over a rock. His body fell hard on the ground He buried his face into the grass and cried out load. Swish of emotions washed though his body, surrounded only by the Rocky Mountains, meadows and lakes. He felt so vulnerable, so small in this universe, yet his problems and secret were larger than the tallest mountains. With no other than just the nature being his witness, Marco let go and cried, at first his tears represented all the anger and angst he had inside him. Then he cried the tears of regret, for his mother Isabel for his grandfather Vin, for himself. He lost track of time, didn't know for how long he had been in this serene place that brought all the tears out and let them go down his cheeks into the grass. He watched a tear drop slid down the grass stem, coating it like a sheer blanket, then disappearing down in the ground with the soil swallowing the lonely teardrop. He wanted to flow like the river, he dreamed of a much brighter future that he wanted to share with Annie, he saw a family of his own one day, with his children by his side, helping him on the farm. But he and his grandfather could go to jail if McGinnis figured out the puzzle. He had a lot to live for; there was so much to do. No one could take that from him. The monster was gone in flesh and blood, but its presence still remained, haunting him in his dreams at night.

He walked down the valley then heard the rumbling noise. The ground underneath his feet boomed. He stopped and looked toward the sun that sat low on the sky, just above the mountain horizon. The rocky peaks turned into a glowing red haze. What a beautiful sight! The unsettling terrain and roar came louder and closer now. He shifted his head to the left when he saw a herd of wild horses running wide through the pasture. The horses were heading straight toward him. He could start running or he could just stand there and see what happens. He opened his arms as if he welcomed the wild, untamed animals into his hear. Marco looked up toward the sky. He didn't feel scared at all, absorbing all the energy, feeling it go through every bone of his body, muscle and flesh. The unexpected presence of the wild horses gave Marco a new hope. The horses passed his motionless body, as if he was just a tree in the wind. The horses didn't stop until they reached the river that flew through the valley. Some lowered their heads; some knelt and drank the ice cold water.

Chapter 16

"Yes?" Trudy Webb raised her eyebrows as she turned her back toward the door. She waited for the door to open, when she heard another knock. She called loudly, "Yes! Come on in, the door is open!" Sitting in her favorite armchair, all she could do is to twist her torso toward the entrance.

The heavy mahogany door slowly opened, and the young man entering the living room said shyly, "Good morning ma'am. My name is—"

Trudy Webb interrupted him, "Marco Savelli," she said with her sharp voice. Marco quietly nodded his eyes mapping the polished hard wood floor.

"What are you waiting for, come and sit down!" Trudy Webb pointed her index finder toward the armchair on the other side of the coffee table. Marco moved nervously before sat down. She studied the young boy's face. His eyes were the same dark color as someone she knew so well. His black, thick and curly hair kept getting into his eyes. The cute gesture he made when a string of curls slid down his forehead and touched his long eyelashes yet reminded her of the soft soul of a man she missed so terribly. Trudy's heart beat into the rhythm of sorrow at the moment. How much she wanted to let him know *who he really was!*

"Ma'am, are you okay? I didn't know whether you recognized me...if you knew who I am." Marco shook his right foot on the luxurious Persian carpet. He suddenly felt embarrassed wishing he cleaned his booths before rushing to visit old Ms. Webb.

"Of course I know *who you are*! I know everything about you. And now, you came to see me, after all these years, for the very first time, we meet face to face, at last." Trudy watched Marco's face as it showed a shadow of confusion, understandably so. She watched him as he rubbed his hands over his knees with his large hands. These were the hands of a true man, with square palms and long, but strong fingers. Trudy Webb smiled at the handsome young man. His shyness only added to his appeal, looking down in front of him, avoiding a direct eye contact with her. He bit his lower lip, and then he brushed his hand through his wavy hair. Every single movement he made seemed to be in a slow, but a beautiful motion. Marco smelled like cattle, and the dirt on his shoes stained the expensive Persian carpet in Trudy's living room, but she didn't mind. "Would you like a cup of tea and something to eat?"

Marco quietly replied, "Yes ma'am. Thank you." He watched Trudy's hand as it reached for a bell standing on a mahogany side table. The golden bell brought a butler to the door and the old, noble lady instructed him with her food request. Marco liked how direct the woman was. She reminded him of his grandfather. He took a sip from a very expensive china tea cup. The hot liquid entered his throat and warmed him up all the way down to his empty stomach. He looked at the sandwiches. They were cut into triangles; each had some type of meat in them. Two were with hard salami and sliced cucumber, the other two had sliced turkey and tomato. He wanted to eat them all, that's how hungry he was.

"Eat as many as you'd like," Trudy replied reading his mind. She reached for a turkey sandwich herself. "What brings you here, young man?"

Marco took a huge bite; he wiped a corner of his mouth. "I came here to ask you a favor, Ms. Webb."

"What kind of favor?" Trudy's eyes played with curiosity. She loved every movement this young handsome man made.

"My grandfather, Vin Savelli, is in a great deal of trouble, Ms. Webb." Marco paused for a moment, "He doesn't know I am here. If he knew, I came to ask you for help...he would have never approved of it."

"I see. I won't tell him you came over, if that's what you want."

Marco lifted his head and looked directly into Trudy Webb's eyes. Despite her old age, her eyes were had a young appeal, blue in color, alert and *gentle*. He hadn't expected that. This gave him the much needed courage to ask her why he came to visit her that morning.

Old Ms. Webb listened to the young, handsome Savelli boy, without interrupting his speech. She quietly but with a great enthusiasm watched his full lips, at they were telling her the heartfelt story. She watched his dark eyes, as they were looking directly into hers, then she shifted onto his hand, as it reached for the last piece of the sandwich.

"And that's why I came over here this morning," he finished as he also swallowed the last piece of bread. A brief moment of silence accompanied them. Marco shrugged.

"There are only two people on this earth that know about this. It needs to stay that way. Do you understand?" She leaned forward in her armchair as if she wanted to emphasis the importance of keeping it a secret.

"Yes, ma'am."

"Good. I'll have some food for you to take home with you." She rang the bell and once again instructed her butler with her request. "Tell your mother I said hello."

✦

"Where have you been? I've been looking for you everywhere." Isabel Savelli had a worrisome look on her face, with pale complexion and fast breathing she grabbed Marco's arm and rushed him to the barn. "Hurry, your grandfather got stomped on by a cow!"

"What? Is he okay?" Marco twisted out of his mother's grip and ran into the barn.

"Grandpa?" He stopped as he saw his grandfather's body lying on the ground. Blood poured from his forehead. Marco knelt over his unconscious body. "Grandpa! Wake up, WAKE UP!" He shook his shoulders, but the old man stayed still on the ground.

"Oh my God!" Marco's mother covered her mouth, tears rolling down her cheeks.

Marco pressed two fingers against Vin's neck. "He has a pulse. Mother, come on help me to get him into the house. Hurry!" They cautiously transported Vin into the house.

Isabel cleaned her father's wounded forehead. A large, purple bruise made its way above his thick eyebrows and expanded all the way to his hairline. His breath was shallow, but steady. Marco stayed by his grandfather's side all night without shutting his eyes. The cow, that kicked him earlier that day, turned out to be sick and had to be shot. Marco destroyed the tortured animal by a single bullet in its head and freed the animal from its madness. He called for help, and they later that evening burned the cow's body out in the fields, in the middle of nowhere.

"Don't you worry, Grandpa, I took care of it," Marco whispered into his grandfather's ear. "I took care of everything today. I spoke to Trudy Webb." He gently stroked his hair and kissed his bruised forehead. He leaned his back on the wooden chair, took of the suspenders from his shoulders and let them slide down his hips. Accompanied by the dim light from the kerosene lamp his thoughts took him to the most beautiful girl he'd ever seen. He played the memory of the sunny day they spent on the Montana meadow in his mind. He heard her laugh again and now, it made him smile. Annie unexpectedly stepped into his heart and he wanted to keep her in, for as long, as he lives. But now he was just grateful for the small victory that his grandfather didn't lose his life today.

☙

Sheriff McGinnis paced anxiously in Newman's bank office.

"Patience," Charles Newman said.

"We searched his house, his barn, we pierced with rakes through the last straw on his farm, and what have we found? Nothing! I know he *is* guilty. I can *smell* it on him!" McGinnis fumed angrily. "I can't arrest Vin Savelli even if I wanted to. *You* need to help me!" He pointed his finger across the room at Charles Newman.

"I...I don't know how I could possibly help you with anything, really," Charles said uncomfortably. He placed his right index finger under his cotton shirt collar, and loosened up the tight space around his neck.

"I know your daughter has been going out with the young Savelli. I need to know what they talk about, where he takes her, what they do...I'm sure he is in it together with his grandfather! Those Savelli men can't be trusted!"

"Sheriff, you are asking too much now. Leave my daughter out of it." Charles Newman raised his voice. "Everyone in this town knows what a drunk Walter Wagner was. Maybe we are all wrong here. Have you thought about it? What if he fell into the swamp behind the edges of town, what if the wolves took him or a bear got to hold of him..."

The sheriff's face stiffened and a deep wrinkle protruded on his forehead. "Nonsense!"

"I'm sorry, Sheriff, but I won't....I can't help you anymore."

A moment of silence entered the room, where the two men stood. Finally, McGinnis placed his hat onto his bald head and smiled wryly, "I'm not finished yet."

After the door shut, Charles slid back to his chair. He'd heard all the bad things the town folks had to say about Walter Wagner. That man was missed by no one. When locals mentioned Wagner's name, they talked about his rage, his mood swings, his foul mouth, and also how much he disliked his father-in-law, Vin Savelli. *A disrespectful rat,* some people called him. But did he deserve to die? The world is full of disrespectful, foul-mouthed rats. Yet, there was no one else with a better interest to take Wagner down than Vin Savelli himself. This remained the simple truth. So where was his body? Why hadn't been the locals themselves looking for him? No one cared except McGinnis. And that's when Charles realized that this wasn't about finding Wagner's body but about revenge between the old Savelli man and sheriff himself. "Oh, God...why didn't I think of it before?" Charles muttered under his lips. "I have to help them, before it's too late." He ran out of his office. He jumped into his car, and took off with the loud noise of wheels spinning on the road. He honked at the slow-moving car in front of him, and then he moved his hand in the air, signaling the car to move over to the side of the road. He stepped on the gas paddle and passed the car.

"Annie? Annie are you here?" Charles yelled in the hallway. He looked on both sides of the wide, hard wood floor entryway, but didn't see anybody. "Elizabeth? Where is everyone?" He rushed to the living room hoping to find the women there, but the house was empty. Was McGinnis already here? Did the sheriff speak to the women before Charles was able to get home? Desperate, he ran outside on the porch. There, in the blinding sun, he saw them sitting on the green grass, talking and smiling. He ran toward them.

"Charles, what are you doing home so early?" Elizabeth said.

"Father? You are all covered in sweat. Are you all right?"

Elizabeth extended her arm toward Charles. He reached for her hand and gently kissed it. Then he sat down next to them. "What's the matter, darling?" Elizabeth asked.

"Has the sheriff been here?"

"No," Elizabeth replied quickly.

"The sheriff? No!" Annie said. "Why?"

"Good. If he comes over to ask you questions, any questions, about the missing person in town—"

"You mean Wagner?" Annie interrupted him.

"Yes. If Sheriff McGinnis asks you any questions about Walter Wagner or the Savelli men – and I don't really know if he is going to or not – but if he is…" Charles took a deep breath. "…this is what you are going to tell him." Charles spoke in quiet voice.

After he was done, Annie smiled at him and hugged him. "Thank you, father."

He looked at her hazel eyes and knew he's made a good decision.

Charles helped his wife Elizabeth to get back to the house, gently leading her through the green lawn toward the front porch. He noticed she was barefoot.

"Are you looking at my feet Charles?" she asked gently. "I just like to feel the grass rub against my bare skin. You should try it sometime. It's so liberating!" She smiled happily. "I am really proud of you, Charles. Even though I can only see through my heart I know the Savellis are good people. Marco brings sunshine to Annie's life. When she talks about him, her entire face breaks into delight and her emotions become alive; the strong passion comes through her voice, her body language, and her laughter. It warms up my heart. Our Annie is no longer a child, Charles. She has blossom into a young lady, and her heart now belongs to the farmer boy. They remind me of you and me, when we were young."

Charles suddenly stopped.

"What are you doing?" she laughed.

"I'm taking my shoes off." Charles rolled up the bottom of his pants.

"Well, how does it feel?"

"Wonderful. Simply, wonderful." Charles replied and kissed Elizabeth's rosy lips.

Annie watched her parents as they strolled through the lawn, under the tall cotton tree, where they finally sat down. She watched their foreheads touching, their eyes and lips together; she heard her mother's laugh and wondered whether she herself will have many moments like these with Marco in the future. Then she looked up at the blue sky and let out a loud sigh. "What will my future bring?" she asked the endless blue blanket above her head seeking a reply, but there was none, that she could hear. She didn't ask what made her father suddenly change his mind about the Savelli family, she knew he did it for the love of her daughter. She no longer feared sheriff's questioning. Annie was ready now, and when McGinnis came to ask his questions, if needed, she knew exactly, how to answer them.

Chapter 17

NIGHT WHISPERER

When I look at the night skies
With my curious eyes
My mind is mesmerized
By all the distant beauty that's letting
My humble soul to open up and see
What kind of place I shall be
A place I long to see.

I find my answer in your heart
Just like the lit stars on the night sky,
Unsettling and bursting and constantly
Changing their glittery colors,
And I know I have found myself in you –
In your heart.

So I let my guard down
And step on the mutual path
To see the endless lit sky with you,
My love.

The whispers at night, all angels come out to see
The happiness in me and you,
When violins play and the universe sways
With such a grace I can't wait anymore
But come home to you, now and forever.

Marco read the poem over and over again. Earlier that day, they were just hanging out, doing nothing at all, sharing their time with Annie's horse Digby. Marco held the horse's reins, while Annie wrapped her arms around his waist, sitting closely behind Marco in the horse's seat. Digby led them through the vast Montana meadows toward the sunset, when Annie slid a piece of paper in Marco's pocket. He wasn't aware of it at that time. Perhaps she didn't want him to know. She hoped to surprise him with her poem, but feared he may not like it. So she decided to place it in his pocket without letting him know. Marco found out about the poem on that very same evening, when he was getting undressed and ready to go to bed. He took off his pants and placed them over the chair when he noticed in the corner of his eye that something fell out of his pocket. He read Annie's poem and couldn't get enough of the sweet words that were meant for him. He smelled her flowery perfume from the paper. He closed his eyes, still holding Annie's poem close to his heart, quickly falling asleep, holding a smile on his face.

As the night got darker, the wind picked up outside and brought the dark clouds, and with these clouds rain came falling down hard, beating on the shingled roof of the Savelli's house. The wooden shutters swung back and forth, slamming against the house and the glassed windows, caught under the spell of domineering wind and storm. A distant scared cry of the horses in the barn remained the only sound of a living being through the hellish night. At first, Marco thought this was just in his dream, a nightmare one of too many he has had, ever since Walter Wagner left his life for good. But when a sharp bladed sound of broken glass slamming against the wooden floor woke him up, he realized the demons also surrounded his house, the only place he had ever known. This no longer was a nightmare of his own imagination. He got up and tried to close the broken window, maneuvering his bare feet on the spilled, broken glass on the floor. He felt the force of the strong, chill wind on his face, when he pushed the window against the latch. And then through the broken part of the glass a gust came through and blew Annie's note from Marco's bed and across the room, somewhere under the wardrobe that stood in the corner of his small bedroom. He quickly rushed to get the most valuable possession in his life, when a throbbing pain entered his body. "Ouch!" He stopped and looked at his foot. A piece of broken glass cut through his heel, immediately releasing drops of bright, red blood. "God dammit!" he cursed and tried to take the sharp piece out of his foot. "There!" Marco held the bloody glass between his thumb and index finger. He hobbled to the wardrobe, leaving a bloody stain behind him on the wooden floor. He knelt and reached with his arm under the furniture, tapping his fingers in hopes to feel the soft piece of paper. When he finally reached it, he placed it on his chest. He pulled out a drawer, grabbed a shirt and wrapped it around his heel. Then, still holding the poem close to his heart, he went downstairs, where he cleaned his wound and applied a clean bandage. Then he got a broom and a bin. He wondered how his mother and grandfather could sleep through such a stormy night. Upstairs, he swept the broken glass, making sure none remained on the floor before jumping back into his bed and falling asleep again with a poem in his hand, now stained with a bloody mark across Annie's text.

The next morning when he woke up, Marco found his mother and his grandfather downstairs in the kitchen. They were eating breakfast. He heard them talking about the damage the storm did last night.

"Good morning." Marco's smile uncovered a row of white teeth.

"Good morning, Magpie!" Vin said sharply, half of his face still bruised up. Saw your window got broken upstairs. We gotta it before the winter comes! What happened to your foot?" He pointed his thick, index finger toward Marco's leg.

"Oh, I stepped on a piece of broken glass last night."

"Are you all right?" his mother asked gently.

"Yeah, I'm fine."

They worked hard that afternoon to remove the broken tree branches that had fallen on the roof and alongside the house. Marco split them with an ax so they could use them later when winter comes. They fixed some shutters that got torn apart and then they brought the horse out and went to town to get the window fixed. All this time, Marco could only think about Annie and her poem. He had memorized it and recited it in his mind. When they finally returned to farm, a sudden pit sat in his stomach. A black car parked in front of their house. As they stepped from the carriage, sheriff McGinnis stepped out of the car.

"Evening!" he greeted the men.

"What brings you here now?" Vin asked hesitantly.

"I won't be long." McGinnis placed his right hand inside his watch pocket in his vest. He paused, before he spoke again. "I have only one question to ask."

"Then ask. What are you waitin' for?" Vin replied disgustedly.

Marco watched the sheriff's hand that covered his gun that was attached to his belt. He felt uneasy, tired and just disgusted by the sheriff's presence. He wanted to run toward the bold, shapeless and sweaty guy and he rip his gun off his belt and make the sheriff disappear for good. All three men stood in a complete silence for a moment.

McGinnis's cold eyes stared into Savelli's. "What did you do with Wagner's body? You know I'll find out sooner or later. Both of you are under arrest!" McGinnis shouted triumphantly.

"Leave the boy alone!" Vin yelled back.

"Can't do that! He has a part in this just like you. You both are going to jail!"

A fight broke and the men twisted their bodies. A fourth one jumped out of the car, and sheriff yelled, "Officer Hanson, cuff the man!"

Hanson ran to the old Italian farmer who lay on the ground and snapped the cuffs around the writs. Then he helped to separate the young farmer from the sheriff and cuffed him, too.

❖

Isabel sat down on the sofa and crossed her legs. With the fingers of her right hand, she brushed on the soft, velvety fabric. She had no doubt the luxurious sofa alone was worth more than her whole house. She looked around as a memory of her past flooded her mind. The room hadn't changed much. How long had it been since she entered it for the first time? The last time she sat on the very same sofa, she was pregnant. They were young and deeply in love. She had dreams and desires, plans that never really came to fruition for her. She touched her stomach. "Oh boy," she whispered, "where did all that time go?"

The heavy mahogany door opened, and a familiar woman entered the living room. Isabel quietly watched as the old woman slowly walked toward her, holding onto a hand-carved cane. Then their eyes met, and Isabel was the first one who shied away.

"Good afternoon," Isabel said and looked timidly at the old woman.

"Good afternoon, Isabel," Trudy Webb answered with her sharp voice.

Isabel watched as Trudy slowly sat down into her armchair. The woman's fragile body almost disappeared in the massive, wide armchair. She leaned her cane on the side and once again stared directly into Isabel's eyes.

This time, Isabel didn't shy away. She noticed despite the aging body, Trudy Webb's eyes still carried a twinkle, just like her mind, sharp and intelligent, hadn't lost anything throughout the years.

"I...Ms. Webb, I came here to ask you for help." Isabel spoke slowly, as if choosing each word with a hesitation.

"Trudy. Or have you forgotten? You used to call me Trudy."

"I haven't forgotten. But it's been so long, I don't think it would be appropriate now, with the circumstances around us."

"What circumstances?"

"Well, you know my father and my son got picked up this morning and were sent to jail—"

"What? They were taken to jail?" Trudy's face tightened. "Have you told him?"

"No. I have never told him."

"Ever?"

"No, Never."

"Well, it's time to let him know now!"

"But they are in jail! Please, please help me to get them out of there. They did nothing. Nothing at all! You've got to believe me! It's all the sheriff's fault. He is the one who came in to our farm this morning and arrested them. Sheriff McGinnis is not a good man!"

"He is the man of law. At least some people think that." Trudy smiled and her lips parted. Two wrinkles, one on each side, framed her face. "But I've never liked him. That man is a nothing but a crook.

"I know it's not your fault. There was nothing you could do to bring my son back. I'm not going to lie; it took me years to come to the realization to accept the facts of the matter that my only son died so young, and that you didn't let me know that you were expecting a baby. I hated you for not letting me know that I have a grandchild. A blood and flesh of my own son, that's in Marco Savelli's veins. And then you married that drunk, that worthless human being...Wagner!"

"But he wasn't like that when we met. Walter used to be a different person, you've got to understand that, Trudy."

"You thought I would never know? That I would not recognize my own blood? Every time I looked at Marco when he came to town, when his body changed and he became a young man, every time I saw him I knew, because I saw my own reflection of a son I used to have..."

"I am sorry, Trudy."

"Why?"

"I should had told you a long time ago. But I was afraid Walter would do something bad to you."

The sincere words of Isabel Savelli brought tears to Trudy's eyes. She instantly wiped them away. She created her persona for the world to see that Trudy Webb is a strong, independent woman. This was perhaps the very first time, someone else saw her cry. When her husband died, she retrieved into her own cave, to grief and to deal with her sorrow. Yet she remained her posture when she was in public. She did the same many years ago, when her only son John died unexpectedly.

"Thank you," Trudy paused, then she took a deep breath before she continued, "I want Marco to know, who his real father was. He was an honest, hardworking man that carried his heart on his sleeve. When your son, my grandson, came over here a few days ago, I felt so much joy in my heart. I thought I had lost it. But Marco brought it back. I feel alive, again. I recognize my own in his strong hands, in the tone of his voice, in his eyes. I won't let anyone, especially that crook McGinnis to do any more harm. You bet your Trudy Webb's word on it!"

"All we have is now," Trudy said gratefully.

She had been relived the day her only son came home to tell her he had fallen in love with a farmer's girl.

"I'm in love, Mother! She is a farmer's girl."

"Your father is going to be disappointed in you. He has higher expectations from you."

With a quiet, contend voice John replied, "He's always had. Father has always had his own visions how my future should be. They are not my visions, though."

✦

When the word got out that both Savelli men had been arrested and were in Wiley's county jail, Annie broke down in tears and could not stop crying. She first heard the news from her own father.

"Annie, there is something you should know." Charles Newman carried a worrisome look. His eyes saddened and his face was lined with wrinkles. He couldn't help himself to feel responsible and guilty at the same time for the two farmers. Annie shut herself upstairs in her room and would come out for two days. Her mother brought her food, but she couldn't bring herself to eat. Then, on the third day she found a way to deal with her grief for the one who was now behind cold bars of the county jail. She knew very well that if Vin and Marco went to public trial, they could be sentenced to death. Walter Wagner once again made himself present.

Chapter 18

The cold, concrete room surrounded by three equally cold walls with a chipped paint and various carvings — the human cries for help and mercy — turned into a place where Marco lay on the ground. The third wall, made of iron bars, let in some daylight but also provided an unpleasant draft at nights.

The officer had separated the two Savelli men as soon as they arrived into the county jail. Marco placed his palm on the shabby wall. "Grandpa?" Marco said in whisper, "Can you hear me?" A pause filled in the air for a moment.

"Don't let them break you, Magpie!" He heard his grandfather's words on the other side of the cold wall.

"I'm scared. For the first time in my life, I am really scared, Grandpa." Marco hoped for an answer, but none came back from the other side of the stone cold wall. He curled up in a ball, with his hands between his tights and shut his eyes, but not his mind. The young and restless consciousness now flooded with thoughts and images from that stormy night that may had Walter Wagner vanish, yet never quite disappear from the Savelli's lives.

✦

The next morning, Annie took her horse Digby to Isabel's farm. The horse's hooves clipped on the dirt road, as Annie held the reins tight in her hands. Salty tears slid down her rosy cheeks as she fought the wind in her face.

She tied the leather rains around the wooden fence, right next to the barns. Digby immediately rested his hind leg by bending his knee and just slightly putting pressure on the tip of his hoof.

"Here, something warm for your stomach." Isabel placed a mug on the kitchen table. The slowly rising steam from the chicory coffee tickled Annie's nose. She sneezed. Her left hand reached into her trousers and from her pocket she took out a folded piece of paper, "Can you please give this to Marco?" she heard herself say. A touch of the warm palm covered right hand.

"Of course." Isabel reached across the table for the handwritten piece of paper. The two women sat in silence, each sipping coffee. Neither tasted the apple pie on the plate in front of them. Then, from the corner of the other room and across the hallway, a snorting pig entered the kitchen.

This made Annie smile. "Hi Spot!" Annie leaned down and scratched the piglet's back.

"He's been looking for his boy," said Isabel in monotone voice.

Minutes later, the women held a tight hug in front of the barn. The cold Montana air made Annie shiver. She untied Digby's leather rains and rushed the horse back on the dirt, rocky road, leaving only a cloud of dust behind her. The sun sat low on the sky, and had a company of several clouds around it. Annie often watched the sky, but this time, the clouds were the judge and the sun was on trial. The clouds floated closer and closer and turned their color red, full of anger and angst, while the sun slowly tried to hide from the horizon, weaker and lonelier. Soon, swallowed by the inevitable red veil, the sun no longer was.

⁕

As he expected, his nights proved to be the hardest. What happened to the bird whose wings were supposed to protect its loved ones? Caged, behind the iron bars, the broken feathers lay on the concrete ground, unable to break free. A deep sigh echoed through the county jail. "Grandpa? What's going to happen to us?"

"I wish I knew... I wish I knew." The cold walls carried the answer to Marco's cell.

"You stay strong, Magpie! You did nothing wrong."
"Neither did you, Grandfather."

✦

Trudy Webb carried a mischievous smile on her face, but not everyone would notice because she covered her head with an oversized, black hat. The see-through netting attached to the top of the hat fell low and across her eyes, showing just enough of Trudy's fierce look to other strangers. She used a very strong perfume on that wet, rainy and humid morning. She tapped the wooden desk with her long nails. Always on the move, she didn't like to be the one waiting for someone else. When he finally entered the room, her smile widened before she spoke to him.

"How long has it been?" he asked her first.

"Too long to count," she replied. The smile instantly disappeared from her face.

"What brings you here now?" Sheriff McGinnis sat on the other side of the desk. He tried to read her eyes, but he found the dark netting and the oversized hat too distracting.

Trudy leaned forward, "I'm here to tell you a story." She spoke with a calm voice, her eyes never leaving McGinnis'. He felt her intensity, yet he couldn't shift his own eyes away from hers. With every breath he took, he inhaled more of the strong, annoying perfume she wore. He carefully listened to every word the old lady said. When she was done talking, she stood and left the room. The very first thing he did was to open his window. Drops of the rain landed on the top of his palm, and the humid air entered the room. Trudy's perfume stayed with McGinnis for the rest of the day in his police station office. Annoyed by it, he splashed cold water on his face, hoping the fragrant flower that kept tickling his nose and throat would wash away. He realized this was just Trudy's way to remind him, that although she left the room, she didn't travel anywhere. At least not until he released the two Savelli men from their cells.

✦

Isabel wrapped her hand around the iron bar. There on the other side she was looking into her father's aging eyes.

"I love you," said Isabel.

Vin quickly wrapped his thick, farm fingers around her small hand. He didn't say a word.

"I remember now," Isabel continued speaking in whisper, "It all came back to me. Everything." She gasped.

Still her father didn't say a word. Instead, he pressed his hand that wrapped around his daughter's on the cold, iron bar.

"Thank you," she said quietly.

A single tear slid down on Vin's weathered Italian skin.

"Thank you, Father."

"I love you," the old farmer said breathlessly to his flesh and blood. He let go of the grip that held her daughter's hand.

A few feet away, her son sat in the corner, on the ground, with his knees close to his chin, his strong, young arms wrapped around his ankles. He listened to his mother's footsteps, coming closer and with each clap of his mother's heel, Marco wished she would raise her arm, and there would be a key, a key that would unlock the heavy iron bars and led them out to freedom. When the last clap of the heel echoed through Wiley county jail, Marco lifted his head and looked at her mother. He quickly got up and took fast steps toward her.

"Mother," he said desperately, lifting his muscled arms through the space between the bars and wrapping them around her mother's slim framed shoulders. Just the cold bars standing between the mother and son, a remainder of the reality he was in at that moment. His mother was the first to let go off the hug. Marco looked at her pale, tired eyes.

"I visited Trudy Webb yesterday," Isabel said quietly.

"Trudy Webb? Why?"

She knew Marco had no idea about the strong ties that he had to the old, wealthy woman. "She is going to help you...us."

"How?" His eyes widened looking deeply into his mother's. "I don't under-stand...how could Mrs. Webb possibly help us?"

Instead of giving Marco any further explanation, Isabel reached down into her pocket and took out a folded piece of paper. She slid her slender arm through the bars, "Here. This is for you. It's from Annie."

"How is she?"

"She came by the house early this morning to deliver this note for you." Isabel pointed her index finger to the folded piece of paper in her son's hand. "Annie misses you, but don't we all."

Caw – caw. A raven announced his presence.

"You could miss it."

"Miss what?"

"Life."

What day was it? What hour? Did it really matter? Time stopped the minute they entered the county jail. Together and involuntarily and with their dignity. But the dignity didn't serve them any good now. Cough prevented him from sleep. He couldn't stop. His entire body hurt. His lungs wanted to push through the ribcage and out of his body, ripping off his old Italian flesh to pieces. He had a terrible migraine. Thousands beating nags on his brain, bred into millions now. His shirt was soaked in sweat. The deep cough invaded his body and held him hostage. The iron bars and concrete floor laughed at his weak, drenched body. Misery was his only company. He slid his tongue over his cracked lips. *Misery* had a new sister, and her name was *Thirst.*

"Magpie, if I confess, they'll let you go. You go and you live your life."

Marco turned his head from side to side in disagreement, but his grandfa-ther couldn't see it.

A cough echoed through the cold, damp walls. Then a moment of silence entered their jail.

"No," Marco said softly, and then he added with emphasis, "Never."

"To hell with your pride, boy! Look where we are. Look where we've been—"

"Don't do it." Marco now pleaded with his grandfather. "Please." *Do not confess.* Marco scraped another line on the wall. Then he crossed it. There were seven crossed lines. How many more is it going to take? *Craw-craw,* the raven laughed, before he opened its wings and flew into the sunset.

Chapter 19

VALLEY OF THE TEARS

If a beating heart
In every human's chest
Represents
The life as we know it,

Then I say that my tears,
The valley of the salty streams,
Are building up and rising
With each pumping beat
Of the heart I was once given,
A heart that represents life,
Yet I no longer feel alive
Despite my heart's drive to beat.

If the truth lies in my eyes
Would it be wise
To let the salty windows of my soul
Drown in that bowl?

And then my beating heart
Can't but stay apart
Because I no longer am
Alone.

My heart has grown
With the only one I have ever known
And for that reason
I choose to live
Because if I pause
I may miss all that beautiful cause
My heart has ever lived for.

Chapter 20

"What do you see? Do you think it's beautiful?" Trudy Webb pointed her index finger toward the framed butterfly on her library wall and said coldly, "Some people find it morbid. It started its life as a simple caterpillar; blossomed into its full beauty and look at it now! It's still pretty, even though it's dead." The old, noble lady's voice had a tone of irony and sadness.

Isabel looked at the Mourning Cloak. The butterfly had mostly dark brown wings. The rims showed bright blue shapeless spots and were completed by beige border. "It looks so peaceful," she whispered.

She buried her memories of John together with his dead body. Young Isabel buried them deep, and thought she would never see a day, when the memories would resurface again. Today all she had buried a long time ago came to light with a single framed butterfly. The image projected in front of her eyes and she relived the warm, Montana summer day once again. They were sitting on a meadow, barefooted, Isabel's dress carelessly unbuttoned, her skirt spread in a circle around her slim waist.

Then John eagerly leaned forward, whispered into her ear, his lips slightly touching the skin on her neck. "Close your eyes," John said as he reached for the wildflower on his right side. He brought the blue long stemmed flower closer to Isabel's nose. A sweet, scented smell entered her nostrils, and she sneezed.

"They are called *bear grass*." John smiled at her, still waving the fragrant flowers in front of her face. "No relation to bears." His smile widened.

She knew well what the wildflower was called. Her own father showed her how to weave a basket from the sturdy stems. Yet, she didn't want John to know. Instead she wanted him to explain. Her father thought her a simple wisdom. Never let the boy you are interested in know you are smarter than him. Boys don't like that. They can get intimidated by your intelligence. After all, you know you are smart, so why not play this game if you really like the boy? Let him lead you, let him be the man. So she did. She let him lead that warm, sunny afternoon. That was the day, perhaps the happiest one of them all, because on that day, John gave her Marco.

"The memories didn't go anywhere, did they? I will never forget that day, I was having a cup of tea outside on the patio. There was a warm, summer breeze. Suddenly I felt this terrible pain inside my body." Trudy placed her right hand over her heart. "This pain entered every bone, every organ, and I knew — *I knew* — my John was dead. I just knew…And then this butterfly floated above my head for a moment, before it fell on the table and landed next to my hand. The butterfly was dead." A single tear came down from an eye. Trudy immediately wiped it off. "John was never a good swimmer. He couldn't keep his breath under water for more than just few seconds…Swimming was his weakness, and this weakness was what killed him." She shrugged. "Since I couldn't bury his body, I at least could frame this butterfly. He sent it to me; I know, he did."

"Every time I look in Marco's eyes, I see John in them, I hear John in Marco's voice," Isabel said with a soft, calm voice. Then, firmly, she added, "Marco is an excellent swimmer." She knew about the dead butterfly that landed on the patio table at the time John drowned. Trudy told her at the funeral. What she didn't know was that Trudy had framed this beauty, perhaps to immortalize its beauty, like John's who died way too young.

Trudy patted Isabel on her shoulder. "Come on, it's time." The two women walked out of the house and out into the wet and cold autumn morning. A car with a driver waited for them outside to take them to the courthouse.

The two defendants stood behind the wooden railing in the small and simple courthouse. One young and strong, the other old and fragile with sweat pouring down his temples, bending at the waist under the amount of cough that had invaded his body. The judge's words seemed like a distant signals coming from far away as Vin watched the judge's pencil thin lips barely move. He wanted to wipe the sweat from his head, but his wrists remained tied up behind his back. He felt a sharp pain in his lungs. His entire body depended on his legs, but the legs decided to give up on him, leaving his body fall down and hit the ground fast. Everything went black, the voices shushed, and there was nothing, absolutely nothing, there anymore. Life paused.

✤

"Father!" Isabel stood up and screamed from the wooden bench. Trudy's arm reached for her and pulled her back at her seat. Other people gasped, but no one really moved.

"Mom" Marco's slips whispered, as he turned his head to the crowd that gathered in the small, and simple courtroom. Isabel placed a white fabric handkerchief over her mouth as she watched her father's lifeless body on the ground.

"Quiet, quiet here!" the judge ordered, but the courtroom became a restless nest of spectators, hungry to see how the next scene would evolve.

Trudy finally stood, unable to watch this circus any longer. "Henderson, aren't you going to help this old farmer? How can you let him lie on the ground like this?" She yelled across the room, deliberately called the judge by his last name. She wanted to intimidate him, to make him look like a fool, which in Trudy's mind he certainly was. After this, the courtroom became an uncontrollable chaos. The audience pushed, making its way toward the lifeless body, some of them wanted to help, while others were like wild predator, vultures ready to snatch whatever they could. The police stepped in, but they couldn't separate the young Savelli who lay on the top of his grandfather's body. A fight broke out and lasted for several minutes. Now even the vultures fought within themselves. The young and strong against the old and weak. The circus no longer belonged to the defendants. And then a single bullet shot entered the scene and the vultures and the defendants and the judge all became quiet. Each one looked at the other, without making a move, then the panic brought on screams and everyone ran for the exit.

✦

"How is he doing?" Annie's dress was soaked and her body shivering, as she took off her riding boots. Her bare feet made a wet print on the wooden floor at Marco's room.

"Here." He handed her a towel and one of his shirts. "Go change, before you catch a cold." He watched Annie disappear in the hallway, then he heard the door click as she shut herself in the only bathroom the farmer's house had. Marco followed her and stopped close, behind the door. He raised his hand and slowly moved it down, in a single motion, as if he was touching Annie's back. "He had a stroke. He got very sick in jail, came down with bronchitis, and all the stress in the courtroom, I guess, it all just came down on him..." Marco said, but he wasn't sure if Annie could hear him behind the door.

Annie slowly opened the bathroom door, her hair still very wet, now curled up into golden rings, that rested over her shoulders and stopped right above her breasts. "I'm so sorry Marco. I really am." She hugged him tight, and Marco let go and gave up, no longer hiding behind his strong face, he let his tears flow down his cheeks, a river of sadness and despair.

"Shh, everything's going to be all right." She nurtured him.

"He lost his speech..."

"But not his movement."

"How'd you know that?"

"My father's mother had a stroke. She lost the movement but never her speech. You can't lose both at the same time, I think. That's the thing about stroke..."

"Did your grandmother ever gain back any movement?" Marco cautiously asked.

"Partially, slowly, never to the fullest though," Annie replied quietly.

"So there is a chance my grandfather can talk again..."

"Yes. There is a high chance of that."

Isabel called them downstairs to eat dinner. No one was hungry, even though the roasted duck smelled delicious. Isabel baked it to celebrate the release of her only son and her ailing father from jail. The judge had little to go by, to hold them any longer behind the cold, iron bars. Even Sheriff McGinnis seemed to swallow his pride, although Isabel was sure McGinnis would never give up trying to figure out what had really happened to Walter Wagner. But, as they say, when there is no body, there is no evidence and without evidence, no one can be held against their will. It's against the constitution, as Trudy Webb said. And so there they sat Marco, his mother Isabel, Trudy Webb, and Annie at the wooden table that Vin Savelli carved out of the old oak tree some years ago. He was the only one missing.

Isabel spoke first. "It's time to tell him."

Marco and Annie instantly lifted their curious eyes, first exchanging their looks, then looking at Isabel herself, then shifting their eyes to Trudy.

"Go on, tell him now." The noble lady insisted.

"Tell me what?" Marco asked unaware of what comes next. He looked at Annie, but she moved her shoulders up and down to let him know that she had no idea what the talk was about.

All eyes were on Trudy Webb now. She cleared her throat, and then she grabbed a sharp knife and made the first cut into the roasted duck in front of her. She chose her words wisely, pronouncing them slowly. "Once, I had a son. His name was John Webb." She paused and placed a piece of the white meat in her mouth. All eyes watched her chew the meat, but only one set of eyes wished, she would just spit it out. Not the duck, the words, of course. "He dated this beautiful girl – unprivileged, yet very beautiful." Trudy looked at Isabel. "John's father, my husband..." Trudy looked up toward the ceiling and then she crossed herself, before she quickly reached for another piece of the roasted duck. "... my late husband, didn't approve of this girl, who grew up on the farm. He had higher expectations from his only son. He saw an educated woman that would challenge his own blood and flesh rather than a farmer's girl."

Marco jumped in, "Mother, where is this going?"

But instead of answering, Isabel reached for a sharp knife and made a fresh slice into the duck's chest.

"Oh come on, Mother...Mrs. Webb...Annie?"

"But with the time he recognized that there is more than just the pretty face and that the farmer's girl is smart and educated," Trudy said proudly, "that her father thought her how to read, and write, and he would bring her books from the library, books so well written that she wanted to know more, and it was the library where she met with John..."

Marco and Annie hadn't touched the food. They watched and they listened.

"They connected like two butterflies in a summer breeze above the vast Montana meadows, uninterrupted, their hearts colliding, creating a brand new life..." Trudy Webb looked deeply into Marco's eyes.

He felt her intensity, his body like an electric storm sent out a tingling sensation through his fingers. He felt nervous and uneasy. His heart started pumping the blood through his veins faster and faster, he knew what was coming next. He closed his eyes. Then he felt her touch. Annie placed her warm palm over his. She wrapped her fingers over his hand, trying to ease his tension.

"John gave me Marco," Isabel whispered.

"What?" Marco looked at her mother.

Her face softened, the corners of her lips now curled into a smile.

"You are my grandson." Trudy Webb announced proudly.

"What?!" Marco couldn't believe it. "Did you know?" he asked Annie.

She quietly said, "No, I had no idea."

"Mother? Is it true?"

"Yes, my son, it's true. I dated Trudy Webb's son when I was young. We were deeply in love. Then tragedy happened and he died. He died before you were born..."

"John Webb was your father," Trudy said as her curious eyes checked on the disbelief in Marco's face.

"Mom? Why didn't you tell me before, why are you telling me now?! For twenty years of my life and I didn't know...Does my grandfather know?"

"Yes, he has always knew. I asked him not to tell you, to protect you...I asked Trudy to never tell you for the same reasons. Walter thought you were his son. But as you grew older, he didn't see any resemblance in you. He often questioned your looks, and then he realized how different you are from him. I think he finally realized you are not his blood."

Marco's face lighted. "I never left like I could be Walter Wagner's son. It all makes sense now."

Trudy Webb reached into her purse that she laid on the empty chair. "Here." She handed him a black and white photograph. Marco observed the man on the picture. He was tall and had broad, wide shoulders. His hair was dark and curly, and it was combed sideways and to the back of his head. He had big, dark eyes and a big nose. His lips were full and shut. He was standing, his left arm leaning on the wooden fence. The sleeves of his white shirt were rolled up, revealing strong forearms. His long fingers held a cigar in his right hand. Marco smiled at the familiar face. He felt the instant connection to John Webb.

"What was he like?"

"He was a man of integrity," Trudy said. "He was smart and kind and optimistic. He had a free-spirited soul."

Isabel went to Marco, wrapped her arms around him, and kissed him on the top of his thick curly hair. "He was a lot like you," she whispered.

He covered his arms over hers. "Thank you," he said with a quiet, calm voice.

Trudy told him everything she thought might interest her grandchild. She uncovered the unanswered questions that had been on Marco's mind. Then Isabel joined in, and Marco felt as if he finally belonged in his own, young, body and mind. Everything on that evening went into its own place. After dinner, he took his horse and with Annie and her horse Digby rode to her house. They placed Digby in the stable, fed him some hay, and gave him a bucket of fresh water. Then they made themselves comfortable in the corner of the stable and they made love to one another.

Later that night, Marco returned to his farm. He entered his grandfather's house and hoped he would find him in a better state. He paused behind the closed doors before he made a light knock on the wooden door. No answer came from the inside, so he opened the door and there he saw his grandfather's body lying on the bed. His face looked peaceful with both of his arms were relaxed and alongside his body. He was asleep. Marco pulled a chair to his bed and carefully adjusted his grandfather's blanket so he wouldn't wake him up. Then he sat down and watched the old Savelli man for a moment in a complete silence. The kerosene lamp made the room dim, and created several shadows on the wall. One from the lamp, one from Marco's sitting frame and one from his grandfather's laying body. It seemed as if the shadows were their audience, watching them back, in silence. "I know who my father is....was," Marco whispered, unaware his grandfather was listening to him. "Trudy Webb and mother told me everything today. I saw John on the photograph and it felt like I was looking at my own image...I feel free now."

A mumbling sound came out of Vin's lips. Marco rose from his chair and tilted his head close and above Vin's head. "Grandpa? Talk to me, please."

"I killed him." The slurred words came out of Vin's chapped lips. He took several deep breaths. "I killed that bastard..."

"I know what you did, Grandpa," Marco replied with a shaky voice. "I know, because I was there, and I saw you. I know why you did it. You wanted to protect me and my mother. You did it because you love us." Tears entered his eyes. He slid his hand over his grandfather's grey hair and kissed him gently on his cheek.

Vin's pale and tired eyes looked at him. "You...you saw me...oh my...?"

"The noise woke me up. At first I thought it was the wind outside, and the rain that poured so hard on the ground and with the wind it beat on the glass windows...but then I heard the noise came from downstairs...I got up from my bed and opened my bedroom door. The noise got louder and louder, and then I heard Wagner yelling at my mother, and then I heard her scream. I was so scared to go down the stairs...." Marco placed his head in his palms. He took a deep breath. "So I jumped out of the window and onto the roof and I slid down, and ran to your house for help..."

"I told you to stay inside," Vin slurred.

"I know Grandpa, I know. But I couldn't just stay in your house and wait. I couldn't do that. I ran back to mother's house, and I hid behind the kitchen window. That's when I saw my mother's body on the kitchen floor. She didn't move. The next thing I saw was you over Wagner's body, and I saw the shovel...I got scared, and I ran away. I ran behind the house, and I climbed up the roof and jumped through the open window back into my bedroom. My clothes were soaked, and my bare feet were covered in mud. The next thing I remember, I woke up the next morning and thought I had a horrible nightmare. I went downstairs, and there I saw my mother preparing breakfast. You sat behind the table, and you drank your chicory coffee. My mind played a trick on me, that's what I thought. Later that afternoon, I went to stables to feed the animals and my foot stumbled upon the bloody shovel you hid in the hay....That's when I realized that what I had seen last night was no nightmare."

"Oh, Magpie...You kept it a secret."

Marco knew that it took all of his ailing grandfather's strengths to speak. He held his hand, "So did you, Grandpa. You kept it a secret, and so did I."

There remained one unanswered question. What did he do with Wagner's body?

"What happened to his body?"

A long pause came from his grandfather's lips. "I fed it to the bears."

Marco smiled and nodded. He understood. He kissed Vin's hand. "You did good. You did really good."

Chapter 21

UNDER THE MAGPIE'S WINGS

Under the Magpie's wings
So soft and warm
New life beings at the dawn.

Hungry and vocal
Yet so pure
The little bird is still unsure.

The wings so small
It cannot fly
But mother bird is there –
So why not try?

With the day the sun is shining
And the little bird is thriving
With the dusk the sun went down,
So did the bird who flew to town.

There under the fine pine tree
The bird found its key
To use its wings
Now strong and feathered
To tie the strings
That used to tethered
All those he loves —
His family he brings together

And now the night settles in
With the moon's nostalgic grin
But the bird is not afraid,
He is smart and so he waits

By the dawn, the moon gets pale
As it exits its way —
Each and every new day
The sky is bright with the sun —
Its eternal light
And so is love, for which the bird
Opens his wings to protect his finest gifts
He's got in the world.

Chapter 22

Five years later, the farm still thrived; the animals produced, and the people who lived there smiled again and lived happily with their lives enriched with a new generation. The little boy ran into his father's arms.

Marco felt an immense joy as his son pressed his warm, little body against his chest.

"Can we go to get an ice cream now?"

"Sure. Let me guess – chocolate?"

"Yes, double chocolate!"

"All right," said Marco as he took his boy's hand into his own and led him to the shop. The child giggled when he handed him an ice cream cone. As they slowly walked out on the streets of Wiley, Marco carried a smile on his face. Life gained new meaning to him and he loved every bit of it. He had Annie by his side, and a family of his own was the best gift he could had ever asked for. The trial of the disappearance of his Walter Wagner never occurred. He had his take that Trudy Webb had something to do with it. He became close to Trudy, who he loved to call "grandmother." She, on the other hand, didn't like to be called that. She preferred Trudy, and so Marco would always tease her about it. They found a common language, and they tried to make up for all the lost years. He would come over with his son, and Trudy would serve them tea and cookies. She showed him family albums, and they spent hours talking about John.

Marco felt a connection to John, although he never met him. John's eyes were now those on Marco's son. The genes undeniably passed on to little George. Annie's father made Marco a bank manager. But in Marco's heart, he remained a farmer. He enjoyed the hard work around the land and animals. Although Vin never fully recovered from his stroke, they found a way to cope. His speech still impaired, he would write his words down, patiently, slowly, but with a dignity known to the old Italian farmer. Isabel settled in to her position of a grandmother. She sang songs to George in Italian language, just like she did to Marco, when he was little.

No one really missed Walter Wagner. His body was never found, and Sheriff McGinnis eventually gave up on the case. Every time he saw Trudy Webb in town, he tried to avoid the old, spunky woman, as his memory was still fresh of her annoying, strong, flowery perfume.

The demon never returned. And so the little, hidden town in Montana's vast prairie continued to live on. So did the magpie, who sat on the pine tree branch, high above the Savelli's farm.

THE END